3/94

SANTA MARIA PUBLIC LIBRARY

D0437196

Discarded by
Santa Maria Library

FIC
Boswell. Robert. 1953-
Living to be a hundred :
stories /
1994.

94   95

Also by Robert Boswell

MYSTERY RIDE

THE GEOGRAPHY OF DESIRE

CROOKED HEARTS

DANCING IN THE MOVIES

LIVING TO BE A HUNDRED

LIVING TO BE
A HUNDRED

STORIES BY

Robert Boswell

ALFRED A. KNOPF   NEW YORK
1994

This Is a Borzoi Book
Published by Alfred A. Knopf, Inc.

Copyright © 1994 by Robert Boswell
All rights reserved under International and Pan-American
Copyright Conventions Published in the United States by
Alfred A. Knopf, Inc., New York, and simultaneously in
Canada by Random House of Canada Limited, Toronto.
Distributed by Random House, Inc., New York.

These stories originally appeared in the following publications:
Antioch Review: "Grief"
The Iowa Review: "Glissando" and "Living to Be a Hundred"
  (also appeared in *Best American Short Stories 1989*)
The New Yorker: "Rain" and "The Good Man"
North American Review: "Brilliant Mistake"
Ploughshares: "The Earth's Crown"
The Southern Review: "Imagining Spaniards"
Voices Louder Than Words: "The Products of Love"
"Others" was a PEN Syndicated Fiction Project Winner.

Library of Congress Cataloging-in-Publication Data

Boswell, Robert.
  Living to be a hundred : stories / by Robert Boswell.
    p.   cm.
  ISBN 0-679-43063-6
  I. Title.
PS3552.08126L58   1994
813'.54—dc20   93-23082
                                                      CIP

Manufactured in the United States of America
First Edition

For Toni
Jade
Noah

CONTENTS

Rain   3

Glissando   25

Brilliant Mistake   47

The Good Man   52

The Earth's Crown   62

The Products of Love   78

Imagining Spaniards   108

Others   124

Salt Commons   130

Grief   146

Living to Be a Hundred   167

ACKNOWLEDGMENTS

The author wishes to thank the Guggenheim Foundation, the National Endowment for the Arts, the Arizona Commission on the Arts, and the Illinois Arts Council for their generous support over the years these stories were written. Thanks, also, to the following individuals:

Antonya Nelson

&

Ashbel Green

and Jenny McPhee, Kim Witherspoon, Susan Nelson, Julie Nelson, Don Kurtz, Christopher McIlroy, Kevin McIlvoy, Pete Turchi, Emily Hammond, Steven Schwartz, Ira Sadoff, Todd Lieber, & David Schweidel.

LIVING TO BE A HUNDRED

Rain

The missing boy—age twelve, gone now forty hours—left the gate open in the low fence separating back yard from forest. It swings wide with the wind, rapping against old fence boards and then the opposing post, striking its latch but not catching, time and again, audible to the nearest searchers. The flat clack of wood, the hollow clank of metal are desolate sounds that make them fear the worst.

Karen Stupka and her friend Orla Figes search together—the sheriff insisted on pairs—hooded in identical yellow slickers issued by the fire department, carrying flashlights from home, rain streaking down their coats, trickling across their faces.

"They said to be systematic," Karen calls to Orla, taking her by the slicker's rubber sleeve, yelling into her friend's hood. They stop before a wall of kudzu, raindrops dribbling off the leaves. The rain's relentless fall through the dense vines makes a sound like the rush of surf. "I don't see how we can be systematic," Karen says. The forest—black, dense, and ancient—covers a thousand Georgia acres.

"Up and back," Orla suggests. "We stick together, right? Up and back as long as we can take it." Orla has a Slavic seriousness to her face and thick, dark brows that converge when she is speaking earnestly.

The forest smells of rain, rotting wood, and something else—
fear, Karen decides. She says, "We can duck under the vines
through there." She shines her light on an opening in the long
fall of kudzu, threads of water sparkling in the beam. She leads,
Orla follows. They live across the street from each other, two
blocks from the tragic home, the swinging gate. It has rained
five of the past six days, the only exception the afternoon the
boy disappeared—a kid interested in mushrooms. His mother
speculates that he entered the woods to add to his collection,
and there is the fear that he may have eaten a poisonous toad-
stool and is now lying among sodden leaves, clutching his stomach, rain pelting his face.

Karen and Orla penetrate the forest a mile away from the
boy's house, an unlikely area assigned to them by the sheriff,
who organized the volunteers according to his sense of their
value. The likeliest areas he gave to off-duty policemen and fire-
men, teaming them with family members, in whom he had no
confidence. Lawrence, Karen's husband, is one of the men at the
heart of the search. He is not a fireman, policeman, or relative,
but he is a big man, young and imposing. His partner is the
sixteen-year-old brother of the missing boy.

The sheriff was dismissing Karen and Orla by sending them so
far away. Karen understands this but has said nothing about it, even
to Orla, forgiving him out of compassion and a sense of the larger
issue of the missing boy, and, too, out of relief, as the assignment
was a partial release from the awful responsibility.

Karen and Orla sweep their lights in unison—rough bark,
green leaves shimmering with moisture, the yellow and brown
of decay, plots of moss, families of mushrooms, a graying branch
sticking out of the earth like a cross. Wind flashes through the
high limbs, treetops bow, leaves fall like rain, rain falls like darkness, and darkness falls like snow, covering everything.

4

Rain

"The rain should keep the spiders down," Karen says. She and Orla share a fear of spiders, which Orla claims is as endemic to women as the fear of snakes is to men.

"I hadn't even thought of spiders," Orla says. "How far should we go before turning back?"

"Farther," Karen says. She is thirty-four, a year younger than Orla and six years older than her husband. She did not marry Lawrence for love, but in the two years they have been together she has come to love him. He is a kind man, not particularly bright, not remarkably foolish—"limited" is how Orla describes him. Now he and Karen are hoping to have children. Orla, twice divorced, has told Karen she will likely spend the remainder of her life alone.

They come to a ravine. The sides are steep and grassy, and at the bottom a shallow stream of water flows slowly through brambles and around large stones. The curtain of rain obscures the opposite bank, sending their beams of light back at them.

"We could turn around here," Karen says, "but this is the sort of place a boy might go."

"You think he could be trapped in this ditch?" Orla steps closer, directing her light at the muddy water. "Down, then?"

Karen shrugs. They hold hands and tentatively step sideways down the bank, their feet sliding in the black mud. Finally, they tumble together into the stream. Orla lands face first but quickly rises, spitting. "I'm not hurt," she announces.

Karen says, "I've lost my shoe."

They stand up together, holding hands again. The water comes to just below the knees of their jeans and pushes them forward, and they go along slowly, casting their lights about. Karen limps slightly, one foot bare. Her light falters, but she twists the plastic lid and the beam is again steady.

The water deepens, and when Orla suggests that they turn

5

back, Karen agrees, pointing again with the light to the opposite bank. Orla nods—they will cover the other side on their way back.

Their first attempt to scale the bank tells them it is impossible—too steep, too slick. They fall forward and slide back into the bottom water.

"Maybe it won't be so steep later on," Karen suggests. Neither wants to retrace their steps: a child is missing.

The ravine grows narrower, the stream deeper, the rain does not slacken. A cold wind punishes the overhanging limbs, pushing against their faces drops of water that sting like pebbles. Orla says something Karen cannot make out. They turn their backs to the wind momentarily, and Orla's warm breath enters Karen's hood. "If the boy's been in this ditch all this time . . ." She shakes her head sadly, her dark hair falling in wet slashes across her forehead and cheeks.

The water has risen now above their knees. Twice Karen falls to a crouch, stumbling over hidden rocks, bruising her bare foot. Orla grabs her elbow each time. The wind rises again—a wall, halting them, making them raise their arms, turn their heads. They hold to each other until it passes.

Orla says, "I've peed my pants." She is laughing, her big mouth opened to the rain. "I didn't see any reason to hold it."

Karen laughs, too. "We may not get out of here until we can swim out."

This doubles Orla over with laughter, wet strands of hair falling free of the hood and lashing the water. "You do it," she says, rising, taking Karen's raincoat by the shoulder. "Pee."

Karen shakes her head. "Impossible."

They stumble forward a few more yards. A gray, leafless tree trails down the bank. It does not give when Karen yanks at the limbs. "You first," she yells to Orla, who obeys. She clutches at the branches and pulls herself from the stream and then up the bank, where Karen soon joins her, weary, muddy, and relieved.

On their knees they rest on the mucky ground. The sky goes white and thunder quickly follows. Karen looks down into the ravine's flow. "We could have been electrocuted," she says. "We could have died down there."

Orla smiles, revealing her long teeth and pink gums. "We could die up here, too." Her chin trembles to restrain laughter.

Karen also feels the urge to laugh, but the flashlight she grips fiercely reminds her of why they are in the forest. "The boy," she says, and Orla nods, somber again. They get up slowly and begin to work their way back through the forest.

Later that night, wrapped in towels on Karen's living-room floor, they drink brandy and wait for Lawrence to return. Orla's towel is purple and emphasizes her paleness, as her bare shoulders emphasize the length of her arms. A gawky woman, she looks all the more so clothed only in a towel. One of her large, bony hands rakes her hair, which, dripping wet, looks better, Karen believes, than when it is dry and styled. Orla wears her hair in a manner Karen finds aggressively unattractive—an old-fashioned puff and curl that belongs on a country-and-Western singer. Wet, her hair at least looks as if it has potential, which makes Karen think of her husband, how he looks best unshaven but without a beard—that in-between stage that raises possibilities.

Orla says, "We should have been terrified in that ravine. Why were we so brave?"

Karen shakes her head to express her wonder.

"Did you find any ticks?" Orla asks, fingering her skull. "I was expecting to find ticks in my hair."

"No ticks, no spiders," Karen says.

To which Orla adds sadly, "No boy."

When Lawrence finally returns, exhausted, his face smeared with mud, he tells them the boy has been found—alive—his leg broken from a fall. He had climbed a tree hoping to see over the forest and determine the way home. The fall could have killed him, but he survived it.

Lawrence removes his shirt as he finishes the story, and it occurs to Karen that they could all three go to bed. Rather than send Orla across the street to her empty house, they could go into the next room and climb into the wide bed. She knows this will not happen. Lawrence sits on the floor to take off his boots. He reminds them that he has been searching with the missing boy's sixteen-year-old brother. "He kept talking the whole time about the trouble the kid would be in once we found him. What a jerk."

Orla adjusts her towel, willing to think of modesty now that she knows the boy is all right. She says, "Some people express their fears that way. Don't be too harsh."

Lawrence peels off his filthy socks. "I suppose you're right. I think I wanted to dislike him." He tosses the socks on top of his shirt. "I know it's unfair—anybody's boy could get lost in the woods. But I kept thinking they must be a screwed-up family, you know? I kept wanting to blame them." He shook his head once, as if to knock the idea out of himself. "How was it down where you were?"

"Rough," Orla says.

"We wound up in a ravine and couldn't get out for a long while," Karen tells him. "I remember thinking we were going to find the boy down there and we'd all be stuck together." This isn't true, she realizes as she says it. It is something like the truth, but not quite.

"I'm going to shower," Lawrence says. "Wait up for me. I'm tired but not sleepy. I want to talk."

When he is gone, Orla asks to borrow clothes, then retracts the request. "If I can hike through that forest, I can certainly run across the street in a towel. Come with me."

"More adventure," Karen says.

They share an umbrella, as the rain has not let up, and walk across the asphalt and through the brown water bordering the sidewalk. Inside, they rub their bare feet on Orla's throw rug, which makes them laugh again.

"We're acting like hysterics," Orla says.

Karen waits in the living room while Orla steps into her bedroom to dress. Through the front window, she sees the matching window in her house, lit, the curtains open. It is the dead of night, but identical windows all along the street are lit; the searchers are unable to sleep.

"Why do you think we were so brave?" Orla calls from the bedroom.

Karen shakes her head, as if Orla could see. Lawrence has just appeared in the window across the way, a white towel around his waist. He is probably disappointed that Orla is gone, Karen thinks. Lawrence does not find Orla attractive, but he likes her to appreciate him. He steps to the window and looks out for several seconds before he spots Karen looking back at him.

Karen parts her towel for an instant. He applauds, and when she gestures for it, he opens his towel, too.

"Why do you think we were so brave?" Orla calls again, entering the room. She wears brown shorts and a sleeveless muslin blouse.

It could happen, Karen thinks. The three of them in one bed. Orla would go for it, she believes, and Lawrence certainly wouldn't object. She understands that it is her decision, and she decides against it. "We had to be brave," she tells Orla. "We didn't have a choice."

"Yes, we did," Orla insists. "We could have sat on our bottoms and cried until they sent a search party after us. I've never really thought of myself as brave before tonight, but we *were* brave out there. You even lost your shoe." She joins Karen at the window, and says, "Look."

Karen turns, fearing that Lawrence is still exposing himself, but Orla is pointing at her rosebushes. "The petals have been blown off, or rained off," Orla says. "Isn't that sad?"

By the time they have crossed the street again, Lawrence has put on running shorts and a T-shirt. Karen thinks of dressing but makes coffee instead. There is something tantalizing about wearing only the towel in front of them. This though Lawrence sleeps with her and Orla shared a shower with her only an hour earlier. With the two of them present, Karen feels a tiny thrill, a flush of excitement, and she does not dress.

Lawrence suggests Irish Cream with the coffee, and Orla likes the idea so much she gets up from where she has been sitting on the floor to fetch the bottle.

"Here we are," Karen says to Orla as she rushes by, "two women home from braving the forest *serving* a man who had it no worse than us."

"Uh-oh," Lawrence says and begins to rise. He is lying on the couch, fully extended, his bare legs crossed. "Need any help?"

"We must like to do it," Orla calls from the kitchen. "Either that, or we have done it so much we don't think about it anymore."

"I think about it," Karen tells her. She sets the tray of cups on the coffee table.

Lawrence smiles tentatively at her. "I'm a dog, right?"

Karen agrees, settles on the floor, aware that her towel opens at the hip, exposing her full thigh. She enjoys this bit of daring.

Orla pours the liqueur into each cup. While they drink, she tells Lawrence about the ravine. Karen is surprised by the details—how, in Orla's story, Karen is the hero, persuading Orla to go into the forest in the first place, goading her to continue, until Orla becomes brave purely through Karen's example. The story embarrasses Karen, because she feels it is untrue.

"You were as much the leader as I was," Karen says.

"But you even let me climb out of the ditch first," Orla says. "You could tell my courage was running low."

Later in the evening there is a moment in the kitchen when Karen, standing alone over a fresh tray of coffee, hearing the voices of her husband and Orla, removes the towel and picks up the tray, imagining the responses from them if she were to walk naked into the room.

Without taking even a step, she retrieves the towel from the floor, covers herself, and hurries into her bedroom, where she finds sweatpants and a T-shirt.

Two days pass, rainy days that force Karen to remain indoors. She and Orla must return to work in a week—Karen to a nearby high school, where she teaches social studies and government, Orla to the community college, where she teaches art. Weeks earlier they decided to throw a party at the end of the summer, and Karen has spent her time indoors cleaning and talking with caterers. Each minute, however, she has been aware of a difference, a subtle shift in her being. If it were physical, it might be that she has begun holding her shoulders in a new way, or perhaps that she had been overweight and is now thin. But the change is not physical, although there seem to be new vibrations along her spine and through her chest—the change has to do with her orientation. Her closeness to and distance from Lawrence, for example, now fluctuate wildly, although he apparently notices nothing new or unusual. And the same is true even with herself, feeling one moment as she has always felt and the next wanting to shed the skin of her present life through some bold action. She has not been the same since entering the forest.

The first guests arrive at nine—the principal of Karen's school and his shy wife, whose name Karen can never remember. The principal is a round man, overweight and bald, round of body and round of head, a bourbon drinker. Usually he talks to Karen about the teachers' union, of which Karen is president, and how he holds nothing against her for the strike of three—now four—years back.

"How's our little organizer?" he says, opening the evening. Karen, rarely at a loss for words, can only smile and shove a bourbon-and-water dangerously close to his face. His wife winces, which is meant to pass as a smile, then looks at the floor and sidles up close to the principal. Her hair, completely gray and in a bun at the back of her head, makes her look a decade older than her round husband. Karen wonders, If the woman were as bald as he, would she look younger? Thinking this and unable to come up with even a single line of small talk, she whirls and calls out, "Orla! Lawrence! Guests!"

By phone, Karen had hired two black women to serve food and drinks. They arrive an hour late, with the house already full of people. One of the servingwomen has brought her daughter, who is sixteen, saying to Karen, "She won't be a bit a trouble." The girl, in a green tube top and denim cutoffs, glares at Karen as if daring her to complain.

In the kitchen, the girl positions herself at the table and sips Coca-Cola, crossing her legs like a boy. Guests mill in and out. The two black women talk in front of the girl as if she weren't there.

"She act like a slut, then I treat her like one," says the mother as she unwraps a platter of cheese. A short, busy woman, she moves with exaggerated quickness. Her skin is light, and the lids of her eyes droop as if in response to some great injustice.

The second woman, much taller, thinner, darker, takes up for the girl. "She's practically a grown woman. You were married by her age and had a child of your own."

"I was never no slut."

Karen does not want this conversation to embarrass her, but when guests look her way she finds herself rolling her eyes, as if to say, "What's a person to do?" or, worse, "What can you do with these people?"

Because she cannot tolerate her own behavior, she asks the women to change the topic of their conversation. Now it is they who trade looks. But all they say to her is "Yes, Ma'am, Miss." This strained formality strikes Karen as an insult, and she quickly leaves the kitchen.

Lawrence drinks too fast, as he often does, and when Karen walks by he throws his arm around her shoulders, jostling her drink and his. "You remember Stella," he says, although Stella is in fact Karen's friend, a young social worker who comes to the high school one day a week. "I was just telling Stella about that boy's brother. I was just telling her how coldhearted he was." Lawrence shakes his head to indicate mystery. "You get to know a person pretty well when you spend six hours out in the woods together."

Karen feels Lawrence is bragging, but Stella smiles in a restrained way, which makes it clear that she considers this a flirtation—a story about getting to know someone in the woods. Karen is again embarrassed and quickly makes her way across the room.

She tries to reach Orla, but the Duncans stop her. They live down the street and are roughly the same age as Karen and Lawrence. Karen thinks that they should all become friends, but each time they get together the evening turns out dull. She sees that they have their two-year-old with them.

"Guess what Bonnie said today," Frank Duncan says, lifting

the little girl until her red, tired eyes are even with Karen's. "Go ahead, sweetie," he says to the girl, who frowns, her lip trembling as if she might cry.

"Dollie keepy," Jane Duncan says, prompting her daughter. "Dollie keepy."

" 'Keepy' is her word for sleepy," Frank explains.

Youth is wasted on the young, Karen thinks, and children are wasted on parents.

"Dollie keepy," Jane Duncan repeats.

By the time Karen reaches Orla, Bob Stefford has cornered her and is arguing about modern art. He is a stuffy man in his forties who wears a goatee and writes a column for the local paper. He believes that he is an authority on all things cultural. "What's false, as I see it—Hi, Karen, nice party—is that modern art exists only for museums. You don't see it in homes. Why? I'll tell you why. For one thing, most of it is too big. I mean the damn canvases themselves. Think about it."

Karen slips away, noticing with a start that the hors d'oeuvres still have not been served. She makes her way to the kitchen, squeezing between the principal and Lawrence, who block the doorway.

"No doubt they are a troubled family," her principal is saying to Lawrence. "The boy and his brother both. Victims, plain as day."

Karen flashes a sharp look at Lawrence, but he seems not to notice.

"Don't you tell me how to raise my own flesh and blood," the short servingwoman says to the other. She holds an open bottle of white wine in her hand and waves it dramatically. The daughter has left the room.

"Aren't you going to serve the food?" Karen asks.

"Of course, we are," the tall one replies, as if insulted. "It's all ready."

"Then serve it," Karen says.

"We just about there," the short woman—the mother—says.

"Serve it now or go home without being paid," Karen tells them. "And don't give me that look."

"What look would that be, Ma'am?"

"You know good and well what look. That wine is for the guests." She is furious and sees that it has begun to rain again, large drops striking the kitchen windows. The rain adds to her anger. "The cost of that bottle will be deducted from your earnings," she tells them.

The women do not acknowledge this statement. Raising platters over their heads, they step around Karen and into the living room. A high wave of noise—relief—greets the sight of food.

"Are these people really our friends?" Karen asks Orla. She has finally managed to reach her, and they huddle in the hall by the bathroom door.

"You're not enjoying yourself?" Orla asks, and Karen is startled to see that she is serious. "Most of them are our friends," she adds. "Except for your principal and that shadow he calls a wife."

Karen smiles, her first genuine smile of the night. "And the serving girls," she says, then corrects herself. "Women. Serving-women." The bathroom door opens as she is speaking, and the sixteen-year-old black girl steps out, eying Karen. She gives a little snort, as if to say, "I should have known."

"Christ," Karen says to Orla as the girl walks off. "In novels, they always say 'serving girls'; I didn't mean anything racial by it."

"Racial?" Orla says. "It sounded more sexist to me." She laughs then. "You're strung tight as a violin."

"I think I'm going crazy. I think I've been crazy ever since we got stuck in that ravine."

"I know what you mean," Orla says vaguely, and Karen hopes she will continue, but a man appears down the hall, headed for the bathroom. Orla slips inside first, without saying anything more.

Before the party is over, Karen has shepherded the only black guest—a middle-aged man who teaches chemistry at the community college and whom Karen hardly knows—into the kitchen and then the living room and hall, putting her hand on his shoulder, trying to find the black girl, as if to prove something. The two women are bartending, but the girl cannot be found.

It occurs to Karen that she herself is no different from anyone else here—just as narrow and foolish. This depresses her. She wants Lawrence now, and leaves the chemistry professor to search for him.

She finds her husband on the couch, talking. As Karen nears, she sees through the crowd that he is conversing with the black girl, who is nodding at him and says, "I know the brother. He act like he the best thing on two feet."

"I wanted to blame the family, you see? Here they are, could be victims of a tragedy, and I wanted to make them responsible."

The girl adjusts her tube top, pulling up each side. "If the family is all like him, they are a sorry bunch. They are. You don't got to feel worser than they do."

Karen examines Lawrence then. He looks bereaved, as if the missing boy belonged to him and were never found. He suddenly excuses himself and crosses the room. Karen hears the door to their bedroom open and close. He will shove purses and raincoats to one side of the bed and stretch out on the other. For Lawrence, the party is over.

"He takes things hard," the girl explains to Karen, as if Lawrence were her friend and Karen the stranger. "He feels bad for every little thing he thinks."

"Does he?" Karen asks her.

But now the girl only shrugs. "He's your husband."

For Karen, the party does not end until after three in the morning. All the guests are finally gone, even Orla, who spent the evening talking to one man and then another, gave it up an hour earlier. Paying the servingwomen—without deducting for the wine—Karen tries to apologize. "I hope this wasn't too awful," she says.

They only nod, not in agreement but in acknowledgment of her half apology. This angers Karen, as they were the ones who were late and who made a scene. The women wake the girl, who is asleep on the couch, and they shut the door silently when they leave. Before their car pulls away, one of them yells, "Bitch!"

Exhausted, Karen cannot sleep. The restlessness is stronger now than ever. She hated the party—every moment except the few she spent alone with Orla. And now she decides that she wants to dance. It seems to her that every good party she ever went to included dancing. She cannot think of a single social event that was any fun that did not have at least one interval of dancing.

Lawrence, though sound asleep, is still in his clothes. She puts on a robe and gently shakes him. When his head rises, she says, "You feel like dancing?" He smiles at her and lets his head drop back to the pillow. "I'm serious," she tells him. "Dance with me."

He makes a halfhearted effort to sit up, raising himself to one elbow. "The party over?"

"Not until we dance. What do you say?"

"Oh, Karen." His head flops back again. "I'm really tired." He yawns as if to prove his honesty. "I'm a dog, right?"

She doesn't answer but rushes out of the bedroom and across the cluttered living-room floor. She bolts out the front door, not bothering to close it, and across the asphalt. Rain is falling lightly, and she has begun to cry.

Through Orla's living-room window Karen spots a light in the kitchen, and through the doorway she sees the kitchen table and Orla's elbows firmly planted on the surface. Orla's head now appears and leans against her arms. She is crying.

It is true, then, Karen thinks, as if what just occurred to her is something she had secretly known. Orla loves her, and she— it must be true, she is standing here in the middle of the night staring in Orla's window—loves Orla.

Before Karen can act on this thought, hands slide across the table from the opposite side. A man's hands. They touch Orla's dark and tangled hair.

Karen turns and runs back across the street. Already she discounts what a moment ago she thought absolutely true. By the time she sees Lawrence kneeling over the stereo, placing the disc in the player, she has pushed the feelings she imagined she had for Orla out of her mind.

Lawrence takes her in his arms. "I just had too much to drink," he says. "It doesn't mean anything." He's worried what she thinks of him.

"I feel wild inside," she tells him.

The music begins and they dance.

The following day, Karen returns to the ravine. The association she makes between the forest and the dark is so powerful that she takes the flashlight even though it's a sunny, humid afternoon.

The sky is clear, although rain is predicted for the evening.

Rain

Once she is past the wall of kudzu and striding between oaks, the flashlight annoys her—the fact that she thought to take it but did not think of its uselessness. She places it in a bed of moss, noting the spot so that she can find it when she comes back.

The powerful desire to return to the forest changes now, as she enters it, into oblique longing—desire without an object. She cannot reconcile the existence of the ravine and the night of wading through water with the existence of the party and the night of dealing with foolish people. And she cannot reconcile the many sides of herself—the woman who married so pragmatically just two years past, the woman who called the black women "girls" and dragged the chemistry professor about like a badge of decency, and the woman who ran barefoot across the street to see Orla. How can all of these people be her?

Daylight transforms the forest. Leafy shadows cast a lacy pattern over her blouse. Birds flitter from tree to tree. Shards of sunlight warm her neck. The sweet odor of rot pervades everything.

She expects to come to the ravine just past the next tree or over the next rise, but it eludes her and she settles on a protruding rock as a place to have her lunch, which dangles from her wrist in a plastic grocery sack. A chicken-salad sandwich and two Oreo cookies, a capped jar of cool water—the ice cubes she put in it have melted. Mosquitoes bother her, and she eats quickly.

A few yards farther into the forest, she steps into a spider's web, the fine netting pressing delicately against her face. She pulls back and swats at the web. The spider makes her appearance, frantically repairing the tear, spreading her fine threads from branch to branch.

Karen is almost ready to turn around when at last she finds the ravine. It is full of muddy water, a fact that startles and frightens her. She removes one shoe and dips her foot into the stagnant, brown water, which is warmer than she would have guessed. She considers a swim, dismisses the idea, considers it again. Then she begins her hike homeward.

Coming here has resolved nothing. She remembers Orla's forehead resting against her arms on the table, Orla crying, the mysterious hands. She marches out of the forest into the afternoon sun and forgets the flashlight.

It is almost dusk. Karen sits on the concrete driveway of Orla's house, waiting. A blue raincoat is draped across her lap. She drinks a glass of wine so as to have something to do. Across the street, Lawrence tromps about making supper. He is still in his work clothes—jeans and khaki shirt. Whenever he passes through the living room, he glances out at her. She can see that he is worried. It occurs to her that he invited no one to the party.

Orla's Chevette finally appears down the street, and as it draws near, Karen can see that Orla has been to the beauty parlor; her hair is once again perfectly awful. When the car has pulled into the driveway and Orla has stepped out of it and paused before the still seated Karen, Karen says, "Why'd you buy this big house? You have three bedrooms and two baths. I don't even see how you can afford it."

Orla laughs and grins her toothy smile. "You're mad because I left the party mess for you and the serving *girls* to clean by yourselves."

"They don't get paid to clean," Karen says, standing. She is wearing the same clothing she wore when they went into the ravine—denim jeans, blue cotton shirt.

Orla bends over to retrieve Karen's glass of wine. "I'm sorry, Karen. I didn't mean to leave you all that mess."

"Make it up to me," Karen says. "Come with me into the forest."

Orla smiles as if she thinks Karen is joking. "Now? It's almost dark. It's going to rain." Just then a gust of wind rustles Orla's skirt.

"It's important to me," Karen tells her. "Lawrence is making dinner for all of us."

"Are you all right? Are you mad at me?"

"I'm not mad," she says, although what she feels is a sort of madness, like being turned on her head. "I just want to go back there."

In the house, Karen steps into Orla's bedroom to watch her change. Orla pulls her blouse over her head, talking all the while about something trivial that happened at the beauty parlor. Those long, thin arms. Then she steps out of her skirt. Her legs, so white, smooth, but though Karen can imagine being attracted to this body she is not, and sees Orla as a giant wading bird. It isn't sex, Karen realizes. She was silly to think it had to do with sex. But it *is* something—some power, some cloud through which Karen now sees the world.

Lawrence is waiting for them on the sidewalk outside Orla's door. "So you're going to do this?"

It isn't clear whether he's asking Karen or Orla, but Orla responds with a laugh. "Make us something hearty, dear. We're going off into the wilderness."

Lawrence produces a smile that quickly vanishes, and Karen realizes that he was asking her—and his question meant "Are you leaving me?"

Karen says to him, "I love you, and I'll be back soon."

As they walk away, Orla says, "Oh," and turns to Lawrence, who has not moved. "I saw those boys today. The one who was missing and his brother—the one you were with."

Lawrence raises his brows. "How are they?"

"The missing boy has a cast on his leg and his brother was getting everyone who was a searcher to sign it. They seemed like nice boys. I thought you'd want to know."

"Yeah," Lawrence says. "I got a thank-you note from their mother."

By the time they reach the wall of kudzu, darkness is imminent. Orla has brought her flashlight and shines it at the opening. "Are we going to try to reproduce this exactly?" she asks Karen. "Are we looking for something?"

"I don't know," Karen tells her. She feels the way she did this afternoon. Once she enters the forest, she loses the conviction that her longing has to do with the forest. But she is at a loss as to what else she might do; and this frightens her, because it seems that she might do anything.

"Let me know what we're up to *some*time," Orla says pleasantly.

A few feet into the woods, Karen spots the bed of moss where she left her flashlight. Beads of water spot the lens, but it still works. "I don't remember your losing that," Orla says, confused and surprised.

Karen tells her about the afternoon hike, then adds, "I've been a different person since we were here, so I came back. It wasn't the same without you. I can't explain it, exactly, but I'm trying to understand it."

"It?"

"*It*—whatever has made me different."

Orla nods, serious now, her dark brows merging.

The forest in the dying light holds pockets of mist. They hover just above the ground like angels. Rain begins to patter against the high branches. Their flashlights sweep the forest floor:

moss, mold, rotting leaves, fallen branches. They move deeper into the woods, the darkness thickens, the rain grows more severe.

Orla stops to slip on her raincoat, a clear plastic thing. Karen slides her arms into the blue sleeves of her coat. They are not talking now, flashing their little lights on mushrooms, weeds, a few wildflowers. Karen feels the mysterious force that has taken hold of her deepen, as if in anticipation. They move forward; rain makes the ground slick.

Finally, they come to the ravine. Although the water was deep only this afternoon, it is now shallow. Blades of grass are flattened against the banks, pointing downward.

"Do we have to go down there?" Orla asks. "I don't see the point." She moves her light over the steep slope, the muddy ledge, and then she steadies the beam and shines it on a knob at the top of the bank. "What's this?" she says, taking a step and kneeling.

Rising from the hardened mud like a tiny stump is Karen's lost shoe.

As Karen accepts the shoe from her friend, *it* suddenly goes away. The vibration, the sense of mystery—gone. How does this make sense? she wonders. How can the loss of a shoe change your life? How can its return change it again?

She feels thoroughly deflated and ready to go home. She turns from Orla without looking up. They walk quickly, retracing their steps. A wind washes across the treetops, and when it passes, the forest becomes unusually quiet.

"Listen," Orla says.

Karen pauses. There it is, the faintest sound, a clack and then a clank—the gate of someone's fence, some other family's, one nearby. Karen turns to Orla. She wants to touch her, kiss her, hold her big, birdlike frame. Shining her light on Orla's pale face, she sees her—really sees her—and hears the distant gate whacking a wooden fence and then its latch, and sees the bad haircut in the transparent rain hood. Orla, listening to the gate, standing still to hear, reveals herself as she did not disrobing. Not a wading bird but a graceless, unbeautiful woman, nearing middle age, childless, living in a house too big for one person. And then Karen sees her more clearly still, not her hair or her toothy smile, but *her*—an astonishing creature, beautiful as a creature as she is not as a woman—and though she looks familiar, she also looks strange, as if life distilled down to its purest thing had been poured into this gawky mold.

The gate's latch suddenly catches, and the silence that follows is the final death of Karen's madness.

"I'm hungry," she says suddenly.

"Me, too," Orla tells her. "I'm starving."

Then Karen warns, "Lawrence is no chef."

Orla laughs. Their lights shine forward at the wall of vines and the leafy opening. They emerge from the woods together, stepping into the downpour of rain.

Glissando

In the spring of 1970 my father and I lived in a one-bedroom apartment over a laundromat in Lordsburg, New Mexico. He was working as a real-estate agent through the mail, and a short-order cook at a truckstop café during the night. He'd also lifted a master key to the washers downstairs and borrowed coins from the machines as the need arose. To allay suspicion, he took only a handful of change at a time.

On my birthday that May he came home hours early from the S & P Truckstop, bursting through our door with a lemon meringue pie held like a newborn in the crook of his arm. His pockets bulged and jangled with coins. Before he said a word, I knew we were about to move on.

"Fourteen, a golden year," he began, pulling my birthday present, a new deck of playing cards, from his rear pocket and tossing it my way. "Time you learned how to drive an automobile," he said. Then he added, "Good catch," as I snagged the deck before it hit me in the face.

Our only vehicle, a motorcycle—and not a big Harley as he had once owned, but a little JSA 125—had no headlamp and was not licensed for street use. He had to take alleys across town and park behind buildings, locking it up with a chain the way you do a bicycle. We hadn't owned a car for three years.

"Birds have wings," my father went on, as if explaining himself to a stranger. "Men got to have automobiles." He set my birthday pie on the couch that doubled as my bed, then fished through the stolen coins in his pocket and withdrew a pair of keys looped together by a noose of electrical wire. "Happy fourteenth," he said, throwing them as he had the cards. "That's your personal set. Pack your things real quick-like, and let's go for a ride."

An hour later, rumbling out of town in a '64 Chevy Bel Air, he told me I would no longer go by Jim Wallace, my real name. I would now answer to Jim Barley.

"Just till you turn eighteen," he said, wiping meringue from his lips and onto the steering wheel, "then you can call yourself anything you please."

Some of his real-estate deals had not been entirely above board, and he had decided to go by his half-brother's name, Louis Barley. Louis had disappeared the year of my birth, but wherever we moved my father put his photograph on top of the refrigerator. It was Louis who gave me a gap-toothed smile every time I opened the door for a Coke or an ice cube or to just stand in the refrigerated air. The new Louis Barley, my father, had gotten a driver's license using his half-brother's birth certificate.

"What should *I* call you?" I asked him.

"Father," he said, "same as always. Nothing's changed but the distance I can put between us and trouble."

A dozen miles out of New Mexico, he pulled the Bel Air onto the shoulder and killed the engine. "Give your old man a hand," he said as he climbed out. In one corner of the car's trunk, among our clothes and possessions, lay a screwdriver and a set of Arizona license plates. "The Chevy gets a new identity, too," he explained. I removed the old plates. He replaced them with the new. My father liked to plan things in detail, and this stop was a calculated part of the trip. Poor timing and bad luck often conspired to ruin his plans, but this evening all went smoothly, which pleased us both.

"One gorgeous night," he said when we had finished and leaned happily against the trunk. The desert rolled around us, dark and seemingly without end. Up above, the sky held an amazing network of stars. He handed me the New Mexico plates, and I sent them whirling over the barren ground. We'd become new people: Louis Barley and his son Jim.

"You got your keys?" he asked me. When I nodded, he pointed to the driver's side.

White specks of gravel embedded in the asphalt sparkled like gems in the Bel Air's headlights. "Hammer that clutch in all the way," he shouted. I obeyed him, then turned the key and the engine came to life. We lurched out onto the dark highway.

He pulled a bottle of rum from beneath the seat, bumping his head against the dashboard as the car jumped forward. "That didn't hurt," he said, rubbing his temple. He began telling a story about his very first drive, how his half-brother Louis had taught him. "Lousy driver himself," my father confided. "Worked the clutch like he was stomping ants."

My heart pounded as we hit fifteen, twenty, thirty miles an hour, the highway all but abandoned—an occasional diesel, a few desert creatures. My father put his hand over mine on the gear shifter, showing me the way down to second, then up and over to third.

"You're getting it." He nodded encouragingly and took another swig of rum. My first time behind the wheel, I took us a distance of one hundred miles.

Alida McGowan was a small and pretty woman whose face would flush red after only a moment in the heat, the pink of her skullcap shining through her thin blond hair, which she cut short like a boy's. She was twenty-two in 1970, ten years younger than my father. Her favorite activity consisted of lying in her underwear on the couch and watching television while sipping iced tea.

She had grown up in Chicago, her father a butcher, but her mother divorced and remarried before Alida turned three. Her second father managed his own grocery, and the third taught high-school French. Alida's mother married her way up the same social scale that Alida, in turn, descended. At seventeen, she ran off with a college boy, leaving him in Los Angeles for an appliance salesman who she abandoned for a ranch hand. His pickup broke down in Arizona where Alida met a diesel mechanic. She was living with him in a Ford van when she encountered Louis Barley.

My father stood five feet, nine inches tall with hair black as a crow's wing. He ironed his shirts and buttoned every button regardless of the weather. He owned a succession of crumpled gray felt hats common to an older generation and wore one all the time, except in bed and in the car. Although he had strong arms, they appeared more swollen than muscular. I wound up with an identical build—something my wife would call wiry when we first met, and scrawny when we broke up.

While Alida looked very much like a modern woman, my father, the brim of his fedora tipped up, looked like a relic. He treated her well, though, and did the same to me. True, he drank, but meanness was not the result. In his whole life he struck me only once. That was later, in Nevada, when things had turned bad between us. To be honest, I'd had it coming.

Our first night out of Lordsburg we slept in the Chevy on a dirt road beside the highway east of Tucson. The following day he managed to drive only a couple of hours. The desert sun reflecting brightly off the hood, combined with his hangover, caused him too much pain. He stopped in Gila Bend, Arizona, pretending it had been our destination all along.

His pretending was something I both recognized and denied. We moved so much, he served not only as my sole parent but as my single enduring friend. I preferred to believe he knew what he was doing, and I did so for a long time, until it was impossible to continue.

Gila Bend was a hot little desert hole, a place to get gas and beer and a second wind for the remainder of whatever long drive you were on. We rented a stucco house painted an aqua color— to look like the ocean, my father claimed. The paint had flaked off in spots, and a gray like bad skies shone beneath it.

He got a job as night clerk at the Space Age Lodge, a concrete-block motel with plastic furniture in the lobby and photos of early space flights on the walls. I joined him behind the registration desk to study. We had left Lordsburg before I finished eighth grade, and he'd decided to compensate by giving me a few lessons of his own. On the evening Alida McGowan stepped into our lives, he had been instructing me in what he called the algebra of blackjack, a complicated system of when to hold and when to ask for a hit.

"No guesswork to it anymore," he told me, shaking his head in awe of such progress as he dealt out five hands. "All mathematical. What you need is a head for numbers, and I think you got one."

At eight that evening Alida appeared at the door. The sun had not set and the temperature outside remained over one hundred degrees. Her face and scalp glowed pink. Her short dress had wide, brightly colored stripes—the sort of thing that would make other people look ugly—and she wore a braided leather strap around one ankle. She lived across the highway with the diesel mechanic but checked in that evening with a truck driver, a big-chested man who wore a John Deere cap.

My father took to her immediately. While the trucker bent over to sign the registration card, my father stared straight into her eyes, smiling and adjusting the brim of his hat. She didn't say a word. If she gave him any kind of signal, I missed it. As she left, she knotted a handful of skirt in her fist as if nervous.

My father lost all interest in the lesson. When I mentioned it, he put his arm around my shoulder and led me outside into the heat. We stood beside the motel's whitewashed walls, and he said softly, "When's the last time you heard of a trucker cashing in before dark?"

He asked as if I'd been with him all those nights at the truck-stop. Then he added, "That any way to leave your vehicle?"

The rig was parked haphazardly in the lot, taking up half the spaces. "Let's give them a call," he said. We went back inside and dialed their room number.

I heard the driver's loud voice coming through the receiver. "Hell, it won't be there more than an hour." The diesel, in fact, pulled out twenty minutes later.

"Jimmy, run over and check on that room." My father watched through the window as the truck rolled over the curb and out into the street. "Stick your ear to the door and see if you hear life."

I ran along the sidewalk that rimmed the Space Age Lodge and leaned up against the green metal door, which was hot to the touch. I couldn't hear anything at first, but I kept listening. It seemed likely the woman had stayed, this being the sort of thing about which my father was invariably right.

In a few seconds she started walking around. Then the television came on. I peered through a gap where the curtains failed to meet and saw Alida McGowan on the bed wearing nothing but panties and a bra, a bottle of dark liquor in her hand.

"Didn't mean for you to pry," my father told me. "Peeking in, that was prying. I only wanted you to listen." He said this seriously but smiling, delighted with the news. "If a customer comes, you say your daddy's fixing an air conditioner and will be right back. Then you call her number."

During the hour he spent with Alida McGowan, no one came to the Space Age Lodge, but I picked up the receiver several times, thinking I would ring them with one phony message or another. Finally, I raced back to her room.

The curtains had been yanked hard so they overlapped. When I pressed my ear against the door this time, I heard the soft and low voice my father got while doing something he enjoyed. I heard her, too, just once, a little laugh that sounded like a wind chime.

Alida moved in with us later that week. My father came home one night with her under his arm, and she never left. Before he even introduced us, she smiled at me and said, "Jimmy always makes me think of jimmying a lock, and Jim makes me think of basketball and the smell of men sweating. You've got a good name. It makes pictures in my head."

I think I fell in love with her right then.

My father got an advance on his paycheck to buy a portable black-and-white Zenith. She lay on the couch half-wrapped in a blanket, drank instant iced tea, and watched whatever came on. We received a clear picture on only two channels, but she never complained—it was not in her nature to object. I often thought she wouldn't even change the channel if I didn't ask to see a certain show.

In all his life, my father had never had anything to do with banks, but as Louis Barley he opened a checking account shortly after Alida moved in. Louis Barley also worked more ambitiously than the man I'd grown up with. Midway through June, the Space Age Lodge promoted him to day clerk. "I'll make manager in another six months," he announced proudly. "Nobody is motivated to stay in Gila Bend but me." He took a second advance to buy an air conditioner for the living room. Before Alida arrived, we'd used just the one in his bedroom and left doors open.

Once he started working days, Alida and I spent a lot of time together in front of the television. I liked to look at her in her underwear, and she didn't seem to mind. As long as my father was at work or asleep she'd lie more or less on top of the blanket, but whenever he sat with us she'd cover herself. She wore white cotton panties, often stained. One pair had a little oval hole just below the elastic waistband. Her bras, white and old-fashioned, revealed less, really, than a bathing top. Later she took to wearing my father's white T-shirts and no bra. She often lay in such a manner that I'd have to leave for a while and go back into my room. When I returned she'd let me know what I missed on television.

Alida told me several stories that summer. The one I remember best had to do with her turning seventeen and her mother throwing a surprise party and inviting the local teenagers, most of whom Alida disliked. They came to her party because of her looks.

"I am pretty, you know," she told me, smiling, her lip curled almost cruelly.

I agreed with her. She described the balloons dangling from the ceiling that had embarrassed her and the stupid gifts—one kid had given her a model car to assemble—and how she had hated all of it. Then a boy handed her a box that jewelry came in, a box made for an expensive ring. Her mother raised her eyebrows and said, "I wonder what that could be." Alida opened it and inside lay a condom. Her mother burst into tears, then shoved the boy in the chest to make him leave.

"I should have been mad at him, too," Alida told me, "but I wasn't."

"Nothing makes you angry," I said.

She shrugged and shook her head as if I had missed the point. "Your mother ever make you miserable?"

"She took off when I was little. We don't know what become of her." I looked at the carpet while I spoke. Talking about my mother embarrassed me. "I only know her from stories I hear."

Alida grunted knowingly. "Your daddy likes to tell stories." She was silent a moment, and then she said, "I could never resist the things my mother hated. My whole life has been an answer to that gift."

I had little idea what she meant, but I smiled and nodded as if it made perfect sense.

A couple of weeks after school began, I got into a fistfight. Clay Lookingpoint, a big kid who was part Indian, said I reminded him of a squat-legged hen. I hit him and broke his nose.

I was accustomed to being new at a school and thought it better to punch someone early on rather than let the abuse build up. I got a swat and was sent home.

I faked the call to my father and walked the short distance to our house. As soon as I stepped inside, I heard a rush of movement. The sliding glass door that led to the backyard opened and closed. "Alida?" I called and walked into the living room. The drapes that covered the door swayed. In the gap between the hem and the floor, an inch of bright sunlight shone on our concrete porch and on a man's big naked feet. As I watched, those feet stepped into pants.

Alida lay on the couch watching TV, the blanket over her as usual. When I started toward the glass door to see who it was dressing on our back stoop, she called my name and patted the couch beside her. "As the World Turns" flickered on the set and she began filling me in. I might have gone on to the door, but she let the blanket fall. She was not wearing panties. She continued talking about the soap opera, lying on her stomach, her pretty white behind out in the open. She called me again and turned her head to face me. "Jimmy, come over here," she said.

I went to her then. When I reached the couch she unbuttoned my pants, slipped her hand inside my underwear, and took my cock into her mouth. She left it there only a moment, then turned back to the television.

"There'll be more later," she said.

I was immobilized for several moments. Finally, I buttoned my jeans and sat in my regular chair.

In another minute, she got up, without trying to cover herself, and went into the bedroom. When she returned, she was fully clothed.

"You're a part of it now, too," she told me. "So you better keep quiet."

I came home from school the next day during lunch. She took me in her mouth again, just as briefly, then used her hands to finish. I was a boy and it didn't take long.

I found if I ran to and from the house during lunch break, I could get back in time for my next class. Occasionally, that same man was there. Alida locked the front door when he came by, having asked me not to unlock it. Once I hid around back and waited for him to emerge—a big dark man without much hair on his head. Alida told me she used to live with him in a Ford van. She told me then about the other men and her fathers. She trusted me with this because of my dedication to her warm mouth and hands.

"Men fall for me," she said, "but they don't fall in love." She was washing at the kitchen sink. I had trailed her into the room, still buttoning my pants. "If I were a man, I'd find a way to love someone like me."

"My father loves you," I said. "He says so all the time." Then I added in a whisper, "I love you."

"Your daddy thinks he made me up out of thin air. He thinks whatever he finds must be just what he was looking for." She dried her hands on a dish towel. I waited to see if she had heard my confession. "And you, well . . ." She rolled her eyes. "You just like to get your rocks off."

I laughed with her at this, although we both knew it wasn't the whole truth.

During the last days of the school year, I ran home and she was gone—along with the TV set and all her clothes. I started to call my father, thought better of it, and went back to school instead. I stayed late, sitting in the gym, acting like I was studying, wondering who was next for her, how far down her mother's scale she'd be able to go. Mainly, I kept a textbook in front of my face, hiding my eyes.

When I finally got to the house, my father stood in a corner of the kitchen making hamburger patties. He had a story about Alida that I might have believed if I hadn't already known her better than he did.

"She got a call from her kin in Chicago. Some family trouble," he told me.

I didn't ask for details. I had been angry with him for several days. It gave me an evil pleasure to see him suffering and pretending.

"You just missed her," he continued. "She asked me to give you her love."

"Sure, she did," I said coolly.

He pretended not to hear my tone. Then he added, "I let her have the TV set. Hell, she'd be lost without it, wouldn't she?" He laughed at that.

Later we discovered that she'd taken both air conditioners, which my father thought unfair. For a long time he remained cross with the memory of her.

We lived in Gila Bend another six months. One day at school—I was a sophomore by that time—my father came to the classroom door and whispered with my Civics teacher. Then he gestured for me. The Bel Air, loaded with our belongings and carrying a full tank of gas, waited for us in the parking lot.

"I've got basketball practice tonight," I told him.

"It'll have to wait," he said. We climbed in and drove out of Gila Bend for good.

My father had one story he liked to tell about my mother.

The two of them had drunk whiskey most of a winter night in a honky-tonk in Albuquerque. Somehow there came to be bets on what songs the piano player would know. My mother wanted to bet he wouldn't know a song that used all of the keys. She had gotten it into her head that no such song existed, having heard it from another piano player way back in her youth—a thing that had stuck with her for years and she was now, finally, going to use.

My father bet fifty dollars. The man played a familiar song— sometimes my father would say "Stormy Weather," other times, "Am I Blue"—and right at the finish, he put his fingers at one end and ran them all the way down the keys before playing the last few notes. My father shrugged and reached for his wallet, figuring they'd been had, but Mother became furious, saying you could do that to any song. "Don't give him the money," she said.

My father knew welshing on a bet was trouble, especially in the sort of bar they were in. He asked the piano player if there was sheet music as proof. He couldn't have read the notes of a scale to save his life, but he studied a few sheets anyway, then returned to the table fifty dollars lighter.

"Called a full glissando, and it was right there in the margins of the music," he told her. "A trick deal, but he took us fair and square."

Whenever he related the story to me, he'd say, "Jimmy, that's why your mother left us. She wanted the kind of life where you hit every note at least once. We can't begrudge her that."

Before Alida McGowan left us, we took two trips together. The first was to see the Grand Canyon, a long drive from Gila Bend even though it's in the same state. My father told me I could invite a friend to join us. The only person I knew very well, Clay Lookingpoint, agreed to come along. We sat in the back of the Bel Air together. For some reason, Clay had brought a notebook and wrote me messages. "She your mother?" asked the first one. I shook my head. Then he wrote, "She rides good in a car." I nodded.

By the time we got to Flagstaff, the sky had grown dark and the Grand Canyon still remained a good ways off. Our stops to pee and some road construction had thrown off my father's calculations. We ate burgers and fries at a crowded drive-in, then we found a motel nearby, although the original plan had us coming back that same night. Our room, made to look like a log cabin, earned my father's scorn. He spent half an hour pointing out the places where you could tell it was just paneling and not really logs. Alida turned on the television and lay on one of the two beds watching an old movie.

Clay suggested that he and I take a walk. Immediately he led me back to the drive-in where we'd eaten. He claimed to have seen girls living out of a VW camper in the parking lot. "We can go there and screw them," he said. Clay had already turned eighteen. While he couldn't have been called handsome, the little crook I'd given his nose made him seem dangerous in an appealing way. Whether I was handsome didn't matter, I knew, as I was fourteen and looked like a boy.

Clay walked right up to the VW camper parked in a corner of the gravel lot and knocked on the sliding door. When it opened a crack, he said, "We're two Indian men searching for squaws." He smiled grandly and laughed.

The person who opened it—a full-grown woman with lines in her face and wrinkles in her neck—said, "Sally, look at this."

Another woman, younger but with a mean look about her, stuck her head out. "They're searching for squaws," the older one said.

"He don't look Indian." Sally pointed at me.

"Half-breed," Clay told her. "We're Yaqui braves."

"So what is your Indian names?" the older one asked.

Clay pointed at his own chest. "Running Deer with Dick Like Horse." He laughed at this more than anyone else.

"What about you?" Sally lightly put her finger on my nose.

I started to say, "Clay Lookingpoint," the only Indian name I could think of. Instead, I said, "Looking Up Strangers." To which Clay quickly added "Dresses" and lifted Sally's skirt a few inches.

The older one slapped Clay's hand, saying, "Why don't you chiefs go down to the bowling alley to search for squaws?" Sally shut the sliding door.

"Hey," Clay called out and hammered against the bus with his fist. "Check this one," he said. The cloth curtains parted and both their faces appeared in the door window. They watched as Clay unbuttoned his pants and peed against the side of their van. The women laughed and shook their heads, then the curtains closed.

Clay and I walked back to the motel pretty happy. "They

wanted us bad," he said. We laughed and repeated the names we'd made up.

Outside our room we found Alida and my father sitting in the car staring straight ahead, saying nothing. My father lowered his window. "Get in, boys. We're throwing this trip away."

We headed back for Gila Bend, nobody talking for a long time. Clay finally spoke. "Why we going back now?"

He asked my father, but Alida replied. "Louis is a prude," she said.

"That's exactly right," my father said. "And won't any of us say what a certain other in this car is."

Nothing but silence followed. Clay lifted his notebook from the floorboard. He wrote, "Her shirt is backward."

Alida's blouse was not on backward but inside-out. The stitching showed. A little white tag turned up at the back of her neck, saying, "Small." I hadn't noticed her shirt. I was worried that she had told him about us, about me and her. But that hadn't happened.

Years later when I finally asked my father about it, he said only that he'd loved Alida as he'd loved no one since my mother, but Alida didn't have the capacity for love. He didn't want to elaborate, and I didn't press.

That was five years ago, the last time I saw my father alive. He wasn't an old man when he died, his thin hair still black as a crow's wing. A cleaning woman found his body in a dumpster outside a motel in Portales. I borrowed a car from a woman I knew and drove down from Colorado to identify the body. The car, a silver Buick with automatic transmission, had to have a new water pump in Santa Fe. Towing and repair cost me two hundred dollars, which made me think of it as mine, and is why I still drive it.

My father had been sharing a house trailer with a sad-eyed woman not over twenty-five. She had peroxide-blond hair but dark brows and a quivering way of talking that reminded me of a dove cooing. She had no real explanation for his death. We sat in the silver Buick while she drank tequila straight out of the bottle, her head pushed against the seat, weeping. "He treated me like the Queen of Sheba," she told me, "like I was nothing but good." When I pressed for reasons someone might want to knife him, she spoke vaguely of bounced checks, gambling debts, poor timing, bad luck.

The one other trip my father and I made with Alida McGowan came about as the result of a letter from the IRS. Addressed to Louis Barley, the letter requested information about his failure to claim money he'd earned taking the census. That was how my father discovered his half-brother was alive and not paying taxes. The form showed an income of a couple of hundred dollars and an address in Riverside, California. The phone company didn't list any Barleys in Riverside, but the drive was only seven hours. My father decided to take the chance. He guessed he might never get another to see Louis.

We left in the early evening. While he drove, my father told us how his half-brother had disappeared.

"You were all of three months old at the time," he said to me. "Louis decided to go see the Caribbean. He was always big on water. Claimed the Caribbean was clear as the sky. He drove down into Mexico and never come back. I wanted to track him, but your mother didn't want to take you south. Afraid she'd get sick and wouldn't be able to feed you. Other things came up, and I never did find him. Years later I tried. After your mother was gone, too. You remember Mexico?"

I nodded, recalling mainly the long bus rides and the unease my father had felt down there, pretending to understand more than he really did.

"I can speak Spanish," Alida said. She began pointing at clouds, scrub trees, cactus, the lights of approaching cars and recited their Spanish names—pretty words that sounded just right, as if those things belonged more to that language than ours.

Near the California line, we left the interstate and headed north on a deserted two-lane that went from Yuma to Blythe. My father pulled off and cut the engine. "I bet you didn't know Jimmy can drive," he said to Alida, then he looked into the back at me. "Got your keys?"

We all three sat in the front, Alida in the middle. I stalled the car on my first attempt to get us moving. "Let her out easy," my father advised. Alida, to soften my embarrassment, confessed that she couldn't drive a stick.

The narrow road had mild curves, and was lit by a bright and persistent moon. I had not driven since my fourteenth birthday, better than a year past, and I had more trouble this time than before, trying as I was to impress Alida.

"Louis and I took a trip like this once," my father began. "Your mother came with us," he told me. To Alida he added, "She had to sit on the hump, too."

"I don't mind," Alida said.

"We'd all been living in Horizon City, Texas, down south of El Paso. A record cold January, snow piling alongside the road. We were heading up to Santa Rosa by way of Las Cruces and Alamogordo. Louis had work in Santa Rosa and thought he could get me on. Can't recall what it was because it never panned out."

"How old were you?" I asked him, keeping my eyes on the blacktop.

"Not much older than you are now. Seventeen, I guess. Me and your mother'd been married about a year. Didn't know it, but she was already carrying you."

Alida said, "That means I was just a kid when this went on."

"That'd be right," my father said. "Louis was driving, stomping the clutch every chance he got, as usual. His old Falcon had a powerful heater, and we drank coffee with whiskey from a thermos. Before long we come to White Sands." To Alida, he said, "If you never been there, picture huge mounds of table salt. Damnedest thing you can imagine. Only, this night, it got three leagues stranger. There on top of the white sand was snow." My father shook his head. "White snow on top of white sand in moonlight just like this." He tapped the passenger window. "Louis about got us into a head-on just staring at it."

As he finished the story, the road wound by a rock hill. Suddenly the Colorado River appeared right beside us, moonlight, blue and beautiful, skipping across the water. "Look at that," Alida said. I had to stop the car to keep from driving into the river.

A little after midnight we finally arrived in Riverside. My father, prepared as always, had directions and drove right up to the address, a duplex with a big porch and a gabled roof. Plywood covered the door and window on one side, but the other half was lighted. We gathered before the good door, the three of us, all a little giggly and proud. The trip, already a big success, now presented us with the opportunity to see a ghost.

My father pounded heartily on the door. A man soon opened it. He stared at us only a second before saying, "Son of a bitch." In the harsh electric light, he looked many years older than my father, his skin a shade of gray—like the hide of an elephant. There was a gap between his front teeth.

"Louis," my father said.

We stood in the doorway for a few perfect seconds. Then a voice called from another room. A thin woman appeared down the hall. She bent forward to look at us, which made me think she had poor vision. As soon as he saw her, my father flinched and quit smiling. He said, "We got the wrong house." He reached in for the knob and pulled the door shut.

On the outskirts of Riverside, we found a seafood restaurant still open. My father ordered lobster for all three of us. He pretended to be in a good mood, although anyone could tell it was an act. "Drove all this way to see a stranger," he said and laughed. He even slapped his knee. Then he called to the waiter for more melted butter, another beer, water, crackers, ice.

I played along with him. I folded a slice of white bread and took a bite from the middle, then peeked through the hole—the sort of thing a six-year-old would do. I wanted desperately to recapture the happy mood we'd had only an hour earlier.

"You're a pirate," my father said, so eager to be jovial that he confused eyehole with eye patch. "Jimmy's a pirate," he told Alida.

She smiled and nodded. "Shiver my timbers," she said and put her arm around his shoulders.

It was after two by the time we returned to the car. We had all grown quiet. I lay across the backseat and didn't respond when my father called my name.

"I wish *I* could sleep," he said to Alida.

She turned to him. Her arm appeared along the back of the seat. Her voice was flat and soft. "Who was she?"

"What business is that of yours?" He spoke angrily, in a hushed tone. "She's someone I never knew. Put it that way. I might have thought I did, but I didn't."

I kept picturing the gap-toothed smile, confusing what I saw with what I'd expected. But the thin woman I remembered perfectly, how she bent over and squinted, as if looking at us from a great distance.

I didn't figure out anything that night, couldn't put two and two together. I understood only that my father was angry and embarrassed, as if those two in the house had conspired to make him play the fool. Up front, he had begun yet another story, the one about the bet with the piano player. Alida glanced into the backseat. She could see I was listening, but she didn't let on.

"Asked the piano man if he had a name for that," my father said. "He called it a full glissando, and I made him write it down. I told her it was right there in the music, but that didn't satisfy her." He shook his head furiously. "Not her. She called me a sap. Truth is, *I* had saved us from a lot of trouble, and *she* had cost us fifty dollars."

Near the Arizona border, he pulled into a rest stop. His stomach was killing him. The lobster, he claimed. "Too rich for my system," he told Alida. As soon as he left, I sat up. I was on my knees with my elbows on the back of the front seat. I watched him cross the dark ground and disappear into the little brick outhouse. The moon had vanished and the night grown dark.

Alida looked at me sadly. She was tired, and bags showed under her eyes. "My parents split when I was two," she told me. "It doesn't have anything to do with your day-in, day-out life."

Her saying this made me angry. It came over me unexpectedly, like a wind that suddenly turns you cold.

"I want you to take care of me," I said, although that didn't convey what I meant. I had unzipped my pants and pulled out my cock. "If you don't, I'll tell him everything."

She clenched her jaw and gave me a long stare. Then she glanced at the door where my father had gone. "Watch for him," she whispered. She bent over the seatback and took me into her mouth. I stayed there no longer than usual. As she

44

pulled away, I felt the hard edge of her teeth. By the time my father returned, I lay on the seat again pretending to sleep.

"Feel better?" Alida asked him.

I didn't want to hear his answer. Something inside me had turned against him. I covered my ears, making his voice sound far away.

Alida cleared out later that week.

Louis Barley's photograph remained on the refrigerator until I swatted it down myself. I widened the space between his teeth with a kitchen knife and sent the photo spinning over the desert. My father never mentioned its absence and never said a word about Riverside. By this time I had figured it all out. I knew my father was a fool. On several occasions I started to tell him as much, but I kept it to myself a long time.

My father got credit cards in his half-brother's name and ran them up past the limits. When the bills arrived, he came to school and we drove off, heading north to Elkwood, Nevada.

Along the way we stopped at the Grand Canyon. We leaned against a metal railing and looked out over the empty space. The sun, setting through clouds, dappled the canyon with light. On the opposite rim, objects shimmered and moved as if made of water. The view held us a long time.

My father put his arm along my shoulder. He had left his hat in the car. A wind off the canyon ruffled his sleeves and lifted his lank and thinning hair. His collar fluttered against his neck, and I realized that his shirt was a size too large.

"Alida would have liked this," he told me, nodding at the canyon. "It's one of the things I could have given her." He shook his head sadly. "Instead, all she got was a TV and a couple of window units."

He said this as if he owned the place, as if that spectacular distance was his to give instead of the thing we stood helpless before. Despite this, or maybe because of it, I believed he was talking for the both of us. I felt close to him. The anger I'd carried for months abruptly left me. I even thought that it might be gone for good.

It didn't turn out that way. He and I had trouble in Nevada. When I turned seventeen, I took off on my own. But that day at the canyon, anger lifted from my shoulders and my heart opened up. I felt for one last time a boy's unsullied love for his father.

Dusk settled in and turned the air cool. We had stayed a long time. The approaching dark ultimately decided us. We got back in the car and headed north toward hardship and misunderstanding and further betrayal, driving as if we hadn't a care, riding with the windows down, wearing our old names.

Brilliant Mistake

The rhythm of the Schwinn was the rhythm of my life, a soulful gliding pulse like Smokey Robinson in "Ooh Baby Baby"—that glottal skip, falsetto slide. The temperature had topped out at one hundred nine, faded to one-oh-four by dusk, would not drop into double figures all night long, heat rising from the asphalt, rising from the vacant desert lots, rippling up into the breathing air, smelling of tar, exhaust, exhaustion. Standing on the pedals, I rode a ribbon through the stalled traffic on Fourth Avenue, rolling up and down the concrete gutters, chugging to Smokey playing in my head, a song I didn't hear so much as perform, pumping hard, then coasting, the horizon going green on its way to black, shutting down for the night, dimming like a bad bulb, while the Schwinn, purple and chrome with a white banana seat, took me across the sweltering town, my T-shirt growing dark with sweat, hair standing thick with it, lips salty from it, on my way to see Karla Lowe, my girlfriend, the summer before high school, a quarter of a century ago.

Karla had an oval swimming pool in her backyard, and her mouth, when shaping her last name, took the precise contour of her pool. "Lowe," I said aloud, tasting it like hard candy, leaning into a corner, my heart working its bump and throb, beating time with the Schwinn, with Smokey, with the bang and bang of being thirteen and being on my bike, Karla Lowe and her pool and her mouth like a pool waiting for me.

Her parents were out of town. I pictured the waters of her pool dark and turbulent, rainswept, as if a deep lake, a river jetty, a quarry, some place where the powers of nature balanced out. Not that I was a stellar swimmer, not even a sound swimmer. I was a flail-and-thrash sort of swimmer—self-taught—a drowning sort of swimmer, but I could hold my breath a long time, longer than Lloyd Bridges, longer than Smokey embracing that "ooh" on the last note, and holding my breath, I would submerge, push off the rounded walls, traverse the pool beneath the surface, coasting, arms arching ahead, chest and hips in a slither, the water like air—a kind of flight.

From my house to Karla's, pumping hard: eighteen minutes, three erections. In the tall oleanders that concealed her yard, I hid my Schwinn, grime from the dirty leaves sticking to my slathered arms like dust to the screen of a lit TV. The music startled me, the fact of it, and the specific line, a black voice really doing it up:

"The purpose of the man is to *love* his woman."

Through a gap in the slats of the high cedar fence, I saw the shindig—big sister's party, seniors in high school shaking their hips by the pool, wearing bathing suits, making faces, twirling their arms like they'd seen on "American Bandstand," while others lounged in the water around the pool's dark lip, sipping drinks, smiling, rolling their high-school eyes. Boys in polo shirts and swimming shorts crowded the keg on the covered patio, gesturing with their paper cups. A couple standing near the fence began to moan, the boy kissing the girl the way I wanted to kiss Karla, his hands roaming from her bare back to the bottom of her bikini, a single finger rimming the wrinkled elastic band.

I entered the yard through the gate. Karla was leaning against a white wrought-iron patio post, her green one-piece lapping up her body, two high-school boys—juniors, maybe seniors—hovering about her, leering like old men, touching her naked arm. She saw me come in, raised her dark brows as a greeting, didn't snub me, not exactly, just let me know she preferred the older boys—for the night, anyway. Which struck me as *why not*, as *okay*, as *fair enough*.

I smiled, stared straight at her, smiled, and yanked off my shirt, stepped to the knobby rim of the oval pool, letting the round rise of the concrete press against my arches, then dove into the shallow water, disappeared beneath the surface, the night suddenly soundless, my arms arching ahead, chest and hips in a writhing glide, coasting, flying.

I came up in the deep end, still cutting through the water, angling toward the darkest corner of the pool, where two girls drank liquor and watched me slither near, ice tinkling in their glasses, shadows moving across their faces, watery light appearing beneath their eyes and vanishing.

"Who are you?" one asked me, her voice friendly, flirtatious, slightly slurred, slightly drunk.

I told her my name, coasting closer, just my name, my chin breaking the water, shadow and light riding my face, sliding up to them, bumping into them, my cheek suddenly against a girl's breast, my legs against their warm legs, my submerged body against their submerged bodies—a miscalculation, a boy just out of eighth grade staring at girls almost ready for college, an accident (sweet accident, brilliant mistake), which would have embarrassed me, but it made them laugh. They thought I'd done it on purpose.

"I know who you are," the girl said, the girl whose breast my cheek had brushed. "You go to East High," she said, her smile a piece of the moon, luminous and white, her wet hair pulled back, falling to her bare shoulders, the straps of her bathing suit loose and looping about her arms like exotic jewelry. "We go to Central," she said. "You're on the basketball team, aren't you?"

"I was on the basketball team," I said, which was true, but it was the junior-high team, the Woodard Termites, and I had been the tenth man on a ten-man team.

The other girl pulled herself from the pool, water cascading down her back and bottom, rippling the dark water. "I'll get us something more to drink," she said, looking at me, brows pitched. "Jack on the rocks okay?"

"Sure," I said, no idea what it meant. The space she emptied, I filled, as if her leaving created a current that sucked me over, a friendly tide. The girl's legs and mine rubbed together beneath the water, this girl I didn't know, maybe four years older than I, who might already have had sex, this girl, her legs against mine, her hair pulled back, her smile the moon. Then Smokey came over the stereo, "Ooh Baby Baby," the song I'd been hearing all day, my song, and I put my hand inside the top of her bathing suit.

Never had I done anything like it before, and I didn't know why I did it then, currents of air guiding my hand.

"Someone will see," she said but did nothing to remove it, smiling again, her hand gliding to my shoulder, touching the cut of my hair at the back of my neck.

Her breast was dimpled from the cool water, the nipple a pressure against the heart of my palm. I did not massage or squeeze her breast, but cupped it gently, as if to feel the rhythm of her heart, or to help her pledge allegiance. Smokey's voice soared, and I felt her knee lift, parting my legs. My face did not touch hers, but there was no space between us, her breathing urgent against my cheek—warm, moist breaths.

Then the other girl returned with our drinks. Squatting, she sat on the pool's concrete rim before letting her legs slide into

the water. I removed my hand, took the glass. Without drinking, without tasting a drop on my tongue, I dipped beneath the
surface and pushed off the wall, coasting through the water,
away from them, the ice in the glass floating up against my
shoulder as it drifted away. I let the glass sink slowly to the
pool's blue bottom.

I surfaced at the other end. Karla was with just one boy now,
her back against the white post, the boy leaning over her, his
hand touching the taut skin along her neck.

"I think I'm going to leave," I said and grabbed my shirt
from the pool deck.

"See you," said she.

I rode the Schwinn, the warm night black now, still triple
figures, but I was cooled by my wet body, pumping hard, water
from my hair running down my cheeks, evaporating, the road
loaded with headlights that grew near, that illuminated me, then
let me go. Meanwhile, the party played on, and Karla was led
inside to her own bedroom, her own bed, the green one-piece
making a wet mark on the carpet, an oval like the pool itself,
like Karla's mouth when speaking her name, the summer before
high school, twenty-five years ago.

And still I think I left at the right time, still I think swimming
underwater with the drink was a good exit, and the girl, a
woman now, must remember our few minutes in the dark of
the pool with the same appreciative mystery that I do.

It is the one perfect moment in my life.

The Good Man

By falling down the stairs and rattling the rail supports, Long wakes Andrea, a displaced Angeleno, who thinks *Earthquake*, and bolts into the hall just as Long arrives there, his swollen face coming to rest on her pale, bare feet. This is how Long meets his wife, who, ten years and two children later, tacks an unopened envelope from First Chicago Bank to the kitchen door and writes a note on the back, terse as a slap, "Good-bye, you shit." With daughter Leslie by the hand and baby Tim cradled in arm, Andrea leaves Long.

He smokes, sitting in boxers at the Formica table beside the dieseling refrigerator, turning the envelope with his fingers—the same motion he once used to roll joints. Inside the envelope is a notice of bounced checks: Fenwick Liquors, Atcheson's Drugs, the Spot Market, Fenwick Liquors, Lou's Barbecue Ribs. Reading it, finally, after crumpling the envelope in anguish, Long decides to quit drinking.

He empties long-necked bottles into the sink, inhaling the odors, which strike him like memories: elusive, sweet, more shadow than substance. He remembers an afternoon from early in their marriage, a Saturday celebration after his first week as a reporter for the *Chicago Tribune*. The sunlight is the color of lemonade, and Andrea, in a stodgy green bikini that almost covers her navel, runs toward him along the water's edge, the beach on Michigan glistening like the feathers of an exotic bird.

"The water's heaven." She tinks her voice—a little rising squeak to end each sentence. "I just love this," she says, tinking, her smile brighter than the sun.

Long, four beers closer to home than she, lies bareback on a rust-colored towel too short for the beach, his skin radiant with love for his wife, blistering with love. "Come here," he says. Stretching his arm, taking her hand, he pulls her to him as if there's nothing to it, as if to say, *Why are so many people lonely anyway?* "You're the best." He kisses her lush, hard mouth. "Drink a beer with me," he says. Then he says, "This is the best moment of my life."

Two years later, the day his story in the *Tribune* runs drunk with errors and he and his editor are fired, Long pauses on the sidewalk and leans against the newspaper building's brick wall, mind clouded by one part vodka and two humiliation, struggling with cigarette and match, fingers shaking. His editor in raincoat and gray hat, an electric pencil-sharpener in one hand, briefcase and a framed photograph in the other, deposits his belongings on the sidewalk and straightens Long's collar, then lights the impossible cigarette. Lifting the frame to show Long, he says, "Jerry, Jeff, James," his finger pausing at the miniature faces of his sons.

"I'm sorry," Long says.

His editor nods, staring into the photograph. "Jeff is squinting," he says sadly. "In every picture we have, Jeff is squinting."

"You won't have trouble finding work," Long assures him.

His editor presses the photograph to his chest. "You will," he says.

Long is wounded by this but does not feel pain. The muscles

in his arms, the sweetness at the center of his chest, the glowing cores of his legs already sing to him the melody of desire, the haunting bodily chorus of drink.

Negrophile, Chicago South Side whore-hunter before he fell on the bare feet of Andrea, Long heads for a jazz bar, remembering the cold afternoon, years earlier, when he had stumbled across Coltrane playing there for almost nobody, blowing like he owned the air, like sound was something wasted by others.

This time, the bar has nothing playing but the stoic talk of bartender and barmaid, both black, who remember him from other times. "Hey," Long says. Bartender smiles. Barmaid takes his elbow, her perfume straightening his spine. There are little bulges beneath her eyes, and her nose is the shape of a squatting child. Long remembers sleeping with this woman a week before he met Andrea. She sits him in a green vinyl booth. "I just got axed," he says.

"I'd say you looked more tanked than axed," she tells him. "Vodka Collins?" she says. "Rum and Coke? Double Henry straight up? Highball? Boilermaker? What day of the month you drinking now?"

"Surprise me," he says, pulling the ballpoint from between her breasts. He scrawls numbers, black and crooked, on a white napkin. "Call my wife," he says. "When I'm good and drunk."

"Pity the girl who be your bride," she says, then makes the call before she brings him anything.

Andrea arrives in jeans and sandals, her little fists in her back pockets, calling him Honey, pleading with him to come home, crying, finally, before he agrees to go. He says, "I've come to no good."

And she, "Don't."

A year and a half later, Long, now a copy editor for Lendel, Lendel, Holmes, & Marquesee, hating the ties and jackets of the young lawyers, the sparkling black shoes of the old ones, takes

The Good Man

Andrea, six months pregnant, to a dinner party at a senior partner's house. The high, gabled windows, the door's low black transom incapacitate Long even before the maid, better dressed than he or his wife, says, "Circle round back. You're forty-five minutes late. Manny is going to hear from me."

"We're guests," Andrea says, but Long cannot enter. Sober, hateful, and intolerably sad, Long lists back to their Nova.

"What's come over you?" Andrea asks him.

"I can't go in there." He speaks into the crook of his arm, leaning against the roof of the car. Believing the heaviness of his sorrow may crush the Nova top, he straightens long enough to crawl inside, face down on the front seat.

Andrea goes around the car, opens the door, takes his head into her hands gently, as if it were an overripe squash, bruised and too soft to eat. "That woman is a foolish bitch," she whispers. "Don't let her spoil our night."

Long, wishing to explain his sudden and impossible fatigue, the weight and dimension of his sadness, forms his mouth into the tent that will become his wife's name, but begins instead to weep, a convulsive breath-sucking stammer of mucus and tears.

Andrea flattens her hands against the back of his head, thrusts against it into the groaning seat. "You bastard," she says. She thrusts again, says, "You shit." She wipes the oil of his hair onto his gray jacket and whips the door shut. "Stay here," she tells him. "Rot here." She walks with the conviction of a priest to the great transomed door, while Long, still crying, nose broken and bleeding, lip split and bleeding, gasps for air.

Before he can stop crying, his chest coughing forward still, with the rhythm of a dying locomotive, the car door opens and Andrea lifts his head into her hands again. "Here, my baby," she whispers, an offering sweating in her hand, leaving a circle on the maternity corduroy. Vodka and water, a tall glass, clear

55

as sanity, its opening a perfect circle. A second vodka rests on the asphalt by Andrea's stockinged foot.

He drinks.

Long hallucinates and searches the bathroom cabinet for cold medicine or cough syrup. He does not leave the apartment, which has expanded now, growing first with his family's absence and now with his delirium, the white shoulders of the bathtub swelling wide as a car, bedroom corners stretching obtusely, becoming almost round, cupboards blooming at his touch—great flowers whose nectar he cannot locate. There are a thousand places in his apartment where the members of his family do not reside, a million places where there is no liquor.

Without Andrea, without his children, without drink, he is clothes without consciousness. Gravity exerts no pull. He wakes screaming, clawing maggots from his arms, and cannot run to the bathroom to puke because he slept on the ceiling. Vomit trails from his mouth, to the bed far below, and becomes his face, a monster of his own making. His elbows bleed from the falls, ceiling to floor.

When he is capable of movement once more, Andrea begins to call his name from the next room at regular intervals. He always looks; she is never there. Shaking himself from madness, he seeks her. He shoves his face into the kitchen sink, inhaling, but the odors of alcohol are gone.

Asleep, he is sane, dreaming his life, talking with Andrea about the noises of furniture, the creaks and ticks, imitating them as best he can, laughing. She tells him the story of her deaf grandmother, who telephoned to say that her soup this morning from a can that is red and white like the flag did not even need water: open, pour, heat. "Isn't this the life?" she'd say, then talk about the headlines, the funnies, the photographs of famous people page after page. "For a quarter. How can you beat it?" she'd say, then read Mike Royko word for word, the receiver on the other end resting on the kitchen counter, holding open the pages of Andrea's cookbook.

In the dream, they talk of the future; in the dream, they have one. Schools not good enough for their Leslie, how they will keep Tim from becoming macho, the route they will drive to California next summer—the endless, banal, and mysterious details of the life Long loves.

He wakes to madness.

Two weeks into a stay of eight at the rehabilitation center, Long receives forms to sign, forms already bearing the slip and glide of Andrea's hand. Her signature stops his breath. She cohabits his dreams—sharing his narrow bed, cursing the thin striped mattress, the antiseptic smell, the gurgle of television voices— but this signature, so specifically Andrea, so deeply real, mocks the dreams and makes his bowels ache.

Long studies the pages for an address, removing paper clips, reading confidential reports of doctors and counselors, who refer to him as "Client Long," coming finally to a stark page of familiar script, labeled Spouse's Report. He reads.

> My husband has been a big drinker since before I knew him. He drinks mornings, afternoons, nights. He was drunk when we married. He lost jobs by working drunk, but he always found new ones. He is a kind man, and people like that. He's not an ugly drunk. When he is a little tipped, he's funny, but that only lasts a while. How he got this way is some mystery there doesn't seem an end to. He loves his children. He loves me. He could have been a good man.

Long tears the report twenty times. A dull-eyed nurse, entering the room with a compartmentalized tray of food, screams at him as if he has threatened her. "You can't read this!" she says, snatching the papers. "You were just supposed to put your name!" Then, "I could lose my job."

He apologizes, smiling, having found, before the nurse entered, the phone number of his wife and an address in Joliet. The nurse gathers the scraps of paper, slips them into the pockets of her uniform, directs an index finger at his wicked grin. "Don't you tell," she says, glaring, then smiling. "I mean it," she tells him, glaring again.

He says, "I need to place a call."

Shaking her head, she says once more, "I could lose my job." Then she adds, "Family?"

He nods.

Long lifts another quarter from the puddle of coins on his lap and slips it into the pay phone. His chair faces the wall. The nurse smokes a cigarette furtively and paces the hallway.

Andrea answers after the second ring.

"Andy," Long says, "how I've missed you, you don't know. How are you? How have you been? Haven't had a drink since you left. Not one. Neighbors called the police. You must know that. Not a drop. Don't you want to see me? Don't you want to talk? I could still be a good man."

"You weren't supposed to see that," she says, angry or embarrassed or pretending—Long needs to see her face to know. He listens while she breathes into the phone, just breathes. "Leslie cut her thumb," she says. "It's not serious. A little nick."

"And Tim? How is Tim?"

"Tim is fine. It's Leslie. She misses you. She doesn't understand."

"*I* don't understand," he says. "Oh, I do, but everything has changed. I'm better. I'm getting better."

"I took them to the beach," Andrea tells him. "It was too crowded. You wouldn't believe the mess people make."

"You miss me," Long says. "You want to give it another chance."

She doesn't say anything, then she says, "I don't know."

"You know," he says. Then he says, "You know."

Long leaves the center in a wheelchair to please the nurses, who claim to be pleasing invisible insurance companies. Andrea pushes the chair, Leslie clutching her skirt. Long holds baby Tim in his arms.

They move to Arizona, where Long has found work through the mail and over the phone as a reporter. The pay is bad; the desert hot. Andrea misses trees, grass, rain, snow, but mostly trees: oaks, maples, birches, the dying elms. Sometimes she misses Long, the way he used to be. In her purse is a scrap of paper, a phone number she dials when she misses her husband and has to let someone know.

Together, they go to meetings. Andrea talks of her happiness and her yearning; Long says it's getting through the morning, if he can just make it through the morning. The others at the meeting say the same things or different things that mean the same.

Tim gets heat rash and no longer sleeps through the night. The doctor gives them a cream and a white powder. They buy a tiny electric fan and attach it to his crib. Leslie breaks her leg falling from her tricycle, a fall that shouldn't have left a bruise. A white cast, calcium supplements.

"I hate to see them unhappy," Andrea tells Long, her voice tinking, as if she might cry. They are in their sweltering bed, the top sheet crumpled on the floor, Andrea in bra and panties, Long in his boxers. Tim is sobbing, the third time he has wakened in the past hour. They lie waiting to see if he will stop. "Children should be happy," she says, touching a strap of her nursing bra, rolling onto her side to face Long.

"I'd been dreaming," he tells her. "When I drank, I would dream about you. Now, I dream about liquor." Taking her hand, he pulls her to him, feeling her resistance: her breasts are aching, her child is crying, her husband dreams of drinking.

Andrea whispers, "I wish you could drink a little. Every now and then." Her breathing is soft, hot against his cheek. The baby's cries grow dim, the tiny fan whirs steadily. "Either that," she says, "or I wish I could love you only a little."

The next morning—a Saturday, the temperature climbing and no work to busy his hands, the blood in his limbs thick with the sweet pain of longing—finds Long driving past convenience stores and slowing, as if he were a teenager trying to get a glimpse of the girl he could not hope to have. Belted into the seat beside him, the cast extending her leg into the empty space under the glove box, Leslie holds a doll to the open window, the wind lifting its synthetic hair.

Long pulls into the asphalt lot of one of the stores, guiding the car between the parallel white lines. One beer, he thinks—a six-pack. "Look," Leslie says, and Long turns his head, only to find that she was speaking to the doll, whose straw gaze is turned toward the clouds.

He shifts the car into reverse.

Long digs a hole large enough to bury them all, then blends in peat moss, liquid fertilizer. He plants an oak, a sapling. The well

around the tree—enormous, perfectly round, seven inches deep—
he fills each night, with a slow run of water from a new green
hose. He steps to the rim. The water reflects the scrawny tree,
Long's face, Leslie's frilly dress and luminous cast as she carefully
steps onto his feet, gripping the creases in his pants. Andrea
stands beside him holding Tim against her hip. Long can see his
son's face in the water, but Andrea's head is turned. Long wants
to see the tree well as a halo. He knows at night it will reflect
the stars. He waits, but Andrea's face does not appear.

He does not drink.

The Earth's Crown

MORNING

Alvin Bishop rises at dawn and faces east, framed in his bedroom window: a thin, naked man, skin the white of flour, hair wild from sleep and as dark as the earth. The sun's light, but not the sun, is visible to him, as if the thing itself were buried nightly beneath the rows of restless wheat, lighting them now so that they turn the blue of water.

Leskirk, Kansas, lies in a part of the Midwest that has little to recommend it but the spectacular flat nothingness that makes it unbearable. Occasionally, a rare spring morning or exceptional summer dusk, the fields stretch to a vanishing point so distant Alvin can see for himself that the world is round. On his best days, he manages to think of these acres of land as the earth's crown.

He stands at his bedroom window, his hands clasped at his crotch, as if to be modest.

AFTERNOON

When he doesn't come home for lunch, Rita calls him at the grocery.

62

"It's the shadow of the elevator," she tells him. "It divides our house in two." She rocks back and forth quickly on their bed, which she has stripped to the mattress pad.

Alvin hears the bedsprings, the frenetic rhythm of her movement, the repetitive groan of the springs.

"It turns our pillows gray," Rita says. "It blackens our sheets. It's the elevator. If you want to be honest about us, you have to start with the shadow of the elevator."

A crackling silence follows. "Rita," Alvin begins, as lost in the silence as he was in her talk. "Did you eat lunch? Did you remember the chili in the refrigerator?"

Rita rubs her hands over the dark stains on the mattress pad. Human stains, she thinks—a whole life could be read by these stains: blood, urine, saliva, sweat, sex. She begins to whistle, stops herself.

Finally, she says, "Darkness, once it touches a bed—"

"I've got a customer," Alvin tells her. A man, his green Peterbilt cap visible over the aisles, stalls at the windows of beer and pop, staring into the cooler.

"So do I," she says and hangs up. She presses her face against the mattress, believing she is about to cry. She feels pressure behind her eyes, but the tears do not come. She pulls the pad from the bed and carries it to the washing machine. There are days when she does nothing but clean.

In high school, sixteen years past, she used to pretend a movie camera followed her around. She and Alvin were the stars of a romantic film. Now she wishes it were literally true, that an invisible camera followed them, and each night before bed they watched themselves, the film making their lives tangible, teaching them how to live, how to recover, slowing their lives so that they made sense.

Without this record, things just keep happening. Their lives quietly slip away.

THE ELEVATOR

Rounded, whitewashed, and fifteen stories high, the grain elevator rises above the puny houses of Leskirk, Kansas, like a bleached column of smoke. Its shadow blackens the western side of town mornings, the eastern half afternoons. During the summer months, the shadow of the elevator reaches the Bishop house by twelve-thirty, dividing it laterally, shadow and light.

At one time they thought of it as summer shade.

EVENING

Evenings are measured by cars and pickups, stray diesels hissing by on Route 96, people coming from or going to Pueblo, a few to someplace more distant: Wichita, Kansas City, Albuquerque, Phoenix. Alvin Bishop knows there are a million places your life can take you. For better or worse, his has taken him here.

He stands behind the short Formica counter of his grocery, stalling. Already he has restocked and straightened the shelves, filled the cooler, mopped the floor, cleaned the toilet. The little accounting he had to do is complete, figures checked and double-checked. He doesn't want to go home. Rita is likely still up. Some nights he can't face her.

He switches off the lights, sits on his stool, resting his elbows on the counter. He thinks this: there must be a hundred ways to ruin your life, a thousand ways to lose the people you love. It seems that life is a thing given to you, then taken back a little bit at a time.

Headlights illuminate the grocery's glass door. A yellow triangle grows on the linoleum as the car approaches. Just as the door is about to turn into a sheet of light, it goes dark instead, filled with a tall, ornate figure, a human silhouette that calls to his mind images of those Hindu gods who have extra arms.

After the startle wears off, he makes out the figure to be a normal human, hands shielding eyes and pressed against the glass, little spots of light at the crooks of the elbows, belly round and distended with child. He unlocks the door and lets in Cheryl Boyer, a black woman, a regular customer.

"Thank god," she says. She has been crying.

"Has something happened?" he asks her, but she raises her slender hand, a signal to wait, then turns to put on a new face. She comes to the store daily to buy the few necessities of a woman living by herself, and to smoke a cigarette. She is almost six feet tall, and five months pregnant, the only black person in Leskirk, a resident of a few weeks duration.

"Are you all right?" Alvin asks her.

"I need a cigarette." Her voice is flat but friendly.

She first came into the store during the last frost of April wearing a gold billowy blouse and red stretch pants. She asked if he would sell her cigarettes one at a time.

"I'm not supposed to smoke at all," she had explained, unembarrassed, "but I've been cheating." She began coming by in the afternoons, the dead hours before quitting time at the elevator, and smoked one or two mentholated cigarettes at the counter while paging through magazines. Eventually, she and Alvin began talking and became friends.

Alvin hands her a True from the open package he keeps for her beneath the counter.

"You know anything about having babies?" she asks him casually, then immediately lights the cigarette.

"There are some things I know about it," he says.

She flashes a smile, white and square, as if he is flirting. "I know nausea is part of the deal," she tells him, "but I get headaches, long ticking headaches. You ever get a tick in your head?" Her long hair falls stylishly to one side. She has dressed as if going to a play or an expensive restaurant—some place far from Leskirk.

"Rita had headaches," he says, "the first few months she was pregnant. They went away after a while."

"Rita is your wife?"

He nods. She inhales smoke. He stays behind the counter, resting on the stool. Each has a hand on the Formica top.

"Are you aware that the nearest television repairman is twenty-five miles from here?" She holds the cigarette upright beside her face. Except for a ray of moonlight entering through the door, the cigarette is the only illumination in the room.

"You have to go to Leoti," he says.

"All day I look forward to a smoke." She takes another long puff. "And eating. I eat a meal every hour—sometimes just out of boredom."

"We have paperbacks," he tells her.

"I've read until my mind is spilling over with little black words. Did your wife gain weight? I can't let myself get fat. I have a terrible fear of obesity. My father got fat."

"Rita lost what weight she gained," Alvin says.

"I've got to have another," she announces, shaking her head, her hair following the motion like a whip. "I knocked on my neighbor's door to see if he smoked. I've been dying for one." She lights the cigarette with her pocket lighter. "I walked down to the café, which was closed."

Suddenly she is crying again. She covers her eyes and turns her back to him once more.

Alvin reaches across the counter and touches her padded shoulder with his hand.

She faces him, wiping her eyes. "It's terrible to be where you don't know one person you can bum a cigarette off of." She shakes her head, her hair once again a whip, then flashes another smile. "Did your wife get weepy when she was pregnant?"

His hand is still suspended in the air, level with her shoulder. He lowers it. "She still gets that way," he says.

Cheryl doesn't like this answer, as if he is ridiculing either Rita or her. She looks out the door as she smokes, one arm resting on her belly, the other at her lips. A new pair of head-lights approaches.

Alvin doesn't want her to think he is making fun of her. He says, "I get a ticking in *my* head sometimes. Feels like a guy with boots is marching in there."

She tilts her head toward the floor, looks at him through the tops of her eyes. Behind her, the door turns white. Light shines through the curls of her hair. He sees that she is a beautiful woman. He hadn't noticed that before. Maybe because she is pregnant. Or because she is as tall as he is. Because she is black. There is no way for him to know.

"You should quit," he says to her.

"Smoking?"

He nods.

She leans against the counter. "Why does your wife get weepy, Mr. Bishop?"

This question turns his throat sour as if he's swallowed acid. He stares at his pale hands on the counter. "She's not well. Sometimes she gets sad."

"Do you have any idea what brought it on?" Cheryl asks, smoke in her speech. "Was she always . . . sensitive?" She smiles a little as she says this.

"I'm not going to say anything against her."

"Who's asking you to?" She dismisses him with a wave of

her cigarette. "I'm just curious. You're my only friend here and I don't even know you."

"For starts, call me Alvin," he says.

"Not too often I meet an Alvin."

She says this as if it is funny. It momentarily angers him. "I could ask some questions of you," he tells her.

"What's to know?" She waves the hand with the cigarette contemptuously. "I got knocked up and decided to have the baby in private."

"Why here?"

"No one I know would ever come here. Now, what's the story with your wife?"

He settles back against the stool, sighs, and begins. "Rita went to college three years before we got married. She reads a lot—used to, anyway. One afternoon she was reading and forgot the baby's feeding time. She was caught up in the book and forgot. I guess she was twenty minutes late. When she went to the crib, Linda—that was my daughter's name—Linda had quit breathing."

"The baby died?" Cheryl freezes for a moment, then the glowing ash of the cigarette slowly descends until it is even with her waist. "Oh, Alvin," she cries. "I'm sorry." Then she adds, "Why would a baby die from eating a little late?"

He shakes his head, but the room has grown darker. He's not sure how well she can see. "Had nothing to do with it. A crib death. The doctor said it just happens. Some babies come with their deaths built-in, and there's nothing you can do about it." The cigarette briefly lights the ribbed fabric of her dress, which is stretched tight across her middle like a forced smile. "I shouldn't be telling you this," he says, suddenly ashamed, "you of all people."

"I asked you."

"You don't need to worry. It's more rare than people realize. I read up on it." Alvin remembers well how pregnant women worry. Rita had to be assured nightly that she'd eaten enough protein, drunk enough milk, that she was doing a good job. He can't imagine a woman going through it alone.

"The long and short of it," he says softly, "is that Rita hasn't been the same."

Cheryl finishes her cigarette. She grinds it with her heel into the linoleum. "Is she getting better, Alvin?"

"Sometimes," he says. "Sometimes not."

She thanks him for the smokes. Before she leaves, she pats his hand, which is still on the counter.

NIGHT

"Alvin." Rita calls his name into the dark house although he is right beside her, his head on the pillow next to hers. "Alvin, Alvin." She says his name not so much out of fear but as if she were naming a whole row of children the same thing. "Alvin."

"What, baby?" He sits up, touches her bare shoulder. Her hair is pulled back and knotted so tightly that she looks continually surprised.

"Alvin, I was thinking about this, and I want you to be the first, Alvin." Her fist taps his thigh. She has slept in her bathrobe, a slate blue like winter skies. The belt has pulled loose. One side bunches at her elbow, leaving a breast exposed. The baby is fourteen months dead. Her breasts no longer carry milk.

"I'm right here, Rita," he says and shifts his weight on the bed, bouncing against the mattress. When she is having a bad night, he has to let her know he is there every second. Bouncing is one way; talk, another.

"I was thinking that children can always be counted on to be children, but grown-ups can't be counted on for anything. I was thinking how adults can be like children when you need them to be grown, and then all the petals drop off your plans, don't they, Alvin?"

"I guess," he says uncertainly. "Sure."

"You fall and you wait for someone to come lift you, and you know what happens?"

"No one comes," he says.

"You know that one. I can drink something now. Do you think? A little water now, and I'll do the rugs." She pauses, thinking. When she speaks again her voice is thin and full of disappointment, but by the end of the sentence there is amusement in it. "What was it we were going to do with the rugs, Alvin?"

It is after three in the morning. She had been dreaming of sleep, watching herself in her dream as she slept, waking in her dark bed without ever waking in the dream. He had been dreaming, too, not of Cheryl exactly, but her silhouette, the odd and intricate shape her body had taken.

"Would you like to hear a song?" he asks. "We could sing one together. 'Never Ending Love'? Or 'Our House'?"

"You don't think I'm ready for water yet, which is what I get for marrying you," she says. There are tears. "Oh, this house is sad. And I sweat. My breasts sweat."

"It's the middle of the night," he tells her, his voice more angry than he intended. "You need to get some sleep, Rita. I do, too."

She slumps back to her pillow, pulls the sheet over her head.

"Don't be upset," he says, but she doesn't move. "I have a never-ending love for you," he sings softly, continuing in a whisper until he feels her body soften with sleep.

The Earth's Crown

MADNESS

Alvin falls in love with Cheryl. They stand on their separate sides of the grocery counter and talk every day. He tells her about the ways his life has turned bad, the mistakes he's made. He tells her how he grew up among a little group of farms known informally as Bishop, Kansas, named for his grandfather. His family was proud of this, but none of them had liked his grandfather. The lies it took to preserve his status proved too much for Alvin to bear. He sold his share of the farm and moved away, though only a few dozen miles. He built a little grocery on the highway.

When he opened the store, he decided, foolishly, not to put in a gas pump. It cost a lot of money initially, and there was something about it he didn't like. But people who are going somewhere don't like to stop more often than they have to. Alvin understands that now. He made a mistake. Then Linda was born. Then Linda died.

He tells Cheryl these facts of his life, and, telling her, he falls in love. In time, she begins to confide in him.

"I'm getting paid to have this baby," she says. "I'm a surrogate." She pauses and touches her stomach, waiting for him to comment, but he doesn't know what to tell her. They are at the counter, each on their own side. She says, "There's this thing living inside me that I both love and hate."

Alvin says, "When grain prices are low, an elevator fills, and eventually the grain ferments. You can smell it all over. If the prices stay low and the summer is hot, the grain may ferment so fast that an elevator will explode. It's actually happened."

"Yes," she says, walking to the door to look at the elevator, "that's just the way I feel."

He steps from behind the counter and stands beside her. The elevator shines painfully white. He says, "It looks like the barrel of a gun, doesn't it?"

"You're imagining," she tells him, then smiles slightly. He touches her cheek. Only for a second.

During the afternoon of the day she begins her sixth month, they make love in the storage room—standing, her elbows against the white-block wall, his hands measuring the expanse of her growing abdomen.

HISTORY

Alvin and Rita met in high school. They dated for two years, nothing more than kissing, touching, and a great deal of talk. She went to Norman, Oklahoma, to study romance languages. He went to Fort Hays as an agriculture major. He lasted seven months; she, six semesters. They ran into each other at the movies one night after two years separation. They made love in his Ford Falcon and got married a few months later. They worked together at the store until late in her pregnancy.

White Woman Creek twists through Leskirk, a measly wash, dry ten months a year, its name the legacy of a Plains Indian tribe whose descendants live now on reservations in Oklahoma and New Mexico. Alvin and Rita often went to a desolate spot in White Woman Creek when they were first married. They made love on a blanket spread across the dry creek bed.

For this reason, Alvin feels ashamed when he takes Cheryl there. That's the very nature of love, he decides. It makes things special, which ruins them.

The night, clear and starry and hot, hovers over Kansas, the horizon still light. Alvin feels the same, as if gravity has let up on him, and there isn't much holding him to the earth.

"No one comes out here?" Cheryl asks him, unbuttoning her blouse. "No one will see?"

"It's not likely." He resists the urge to tell her he's come here before for the same purpose.

Stalks of corn border the creek bed in rows, like spectators. Cheryl and Alvin lie across the blanket at an angle, so that it becomes a white diamond, whiter even than his skin. The surrounding stalks of corn genuflect now and then to an invisible, gusting wind. Eventually, she kneels. They make love.

"Had you ever slept with a black woman before?" she asks him.

"I'd never touched a black woman before," he says.

"My mother is white," she tells him.

He doesn't reply. They don't talk again until they are finished, lying side by side on the blanket, beneath a sky now filled with stars.

"You don't like to talk while we do it, do you?" She runs her hand across his bare chest. "Rita doesn't talk when you make love to her?"

"What kind of question is that?"

"Perfectly good question. Do you sleep with your wife or not?"

"Not for a long time," he says.

She puts her lips to his ear and whispers, "You should." She turns and lies flat on her back. "If you don't, I'm not going to do this anymore."

"I don't get it."

Cheryl lifts her hands, opening her arms, as if she is about to conduct an orchestra. "She's your wife. You should sleep with her. You should make love with your wife." She folds her arms across her chest, takes her breasts in her hands. "I had tiny breasts before I was pregnant. I was always self-conscious about them. I refused to let boys see me in a bathing suit when I was in high school." She laughs. "Now, here I am fat as the moon and naked in a creek bed with some white man, and I don't feel self-conscious at all." She sits up, with some difficulty. "You want to know a secret?"

"Yeah," he says, "I'd like that." A little wind blows over them, rustling the dry grass along the bank.

"When my father was in college, he injured himself. He twisted his knee during basketball practice. The team's physician was called in, and my father asked how it looked. You know what that man told him? He said, 'If you were a horse, I'd shoot you.' Can you imagine saying that to a person?" She lifts her hair from her neck and looks up into the dark sky, as if the stars might answer her.

LOVE

By the end of Cheryl's seventh month, she can no longer make love. Still they meet nightly—to talk, to hold hands, to watch the ghosts her television produces. Occasionally, they touch each other. Most nights they merely lie side by side in Cheryl's bed and say almost nothing.

Twice, they fight. Once because he asks where she grew up. He knows she came to Leskirk from Tulsa, but she doesn't sound to Alvin like an Okie.

"You mean I don't sound like an Okie nigger, don't you?" she accuses.

He tells her no, but they fight anyway.

The second time is when he confesses that he still has not made love with Rita.

"Then leave," she says.

He wants to know why.

"Because you're not the man I thought you were."

Alvin knows he has done bad things in his life. He knows some would count sleeping with Cheryl among them. He is certain many would mark it as the worst. He considers making love with his wife in order to please his lover as the worst. He wonders how much worse a human can do.

"Alvin," Rita says. "You love me, Alvin?" They are in bed. He has crawled on top of her. "Alvin," she says and wraps her arms around his head, clutching him against her chest. "I'm afraid of this," she whispers, then kisses him. "I'm afraid of this," she whispers again.

He wants to concentrate on her worry, but what he thinks of is Cheryl, who always talks during sex. This shames him. "There's no reason to be afraid," he tells his wife.

She squeezes shut her eyes. Near the end, she whispers, "We could do a child."

"Is that why you're scared?" he asks.

"That's most of it," she tells him.

Afterwards, she rests her head in the crook of his arm. They lie together for several minutes, quiet and close, as they had lain many times before the trouble. He spoils it, but he wants to know.

"What's the rest of it?" he says. "Why else are you afraid to make love with me?"

She says, "I've been kind of crazy, haven't I? I have. I've been a little crazy, Alvin. Don't you think?"

"You've been upset," he says. "You've been sick."

She moves her hands in the air as if inviting someone to join them. She says, "I know you've been seeing somebody."

Alvin's breath catches in his throat. For several seconds, neither of them does anything but breathe.

"I thought I was already certain," she tells him. "Then tonight. Then now. I'm completely sure because of now." She is quiet another moment before she says, "I get confused, except for this one thing—I know. If you don't stop seeing her, I'll leave you."

The night drags on into morning. Alvin sleeps fitfully. He thinks of the day they came home from the Leoti hospital without their daughter. How still and blank the air had become, how cruel the bright colors of toys had become, how suddenly and unexpectedly an ordinary life became extraordinary and awful, and then, with incredible swiftness, ordinary again, full of ordinary madness and anger, and long ticking months of ordinary sorrow.

He lies in bed with his weeping wife and he weeps.

RECKONING

Alvin stays home and makes Rita breakfast: toast, scrambled eggs, bacon. He intends to go to the grocery before lunch, but he watches television with Rita a while and becomes sleepy. The store remains closed. He spends the afternoon in their bedroom, watching the shadow of the elevator turn the walls dark, examining the simple facts of his life: Rita is sick but she will likely get better. Even if she doesn't, she deserves his love. Cheryl will be gone in little more than a month. Even if he decides he is willing to go with her, there is less than half a chance she will want him along.

It is there in the darkening room that he decides to stop seeing Cheryl. He will give her a carton of cigarettes and say good-bye. He will kiss her slender hand and wish her good luck.

The decision brings a lightness to his chest and shoulders, to his weary heart.

The Earth's Crown

LOVE

Why then does he find himself the following night in Cheryl's wide bed? Why does he listen to her soft breathing and fill a spiral notebook with words of love for her? Why does he lay his hand on her belly to feel the bump and kick of a baby that is not his and is not even hers? Why is it when he stares out her window at the wheat fields he sees the crown of the earth, shining and golden in the dying sunlight?

Because there are ten thousand ways to ruin your life, a million ways to lose the people you love. And this is the way Alvin has chosen. This one is his.

The Products of Love

When I was nineteen and first married, my wife said something I still think about today, twenty years later. "You believe love is beautiful like sunlight," she told me, "but it's more like the wind—you see only its consequences." On a grassy lawn at the center of the university, we sat with our legs intertwined, speaking seriously. We had married a month after we'd met and treated our romance with solemn reverence. "You confuse love with the effects it produces," she said.

My marriage broke up a long time ago. I begin here because I'm convinced this story is as much about the products of love as it is about love.

Paula and Eugene Loroun moved into my neighborhood three years ago, a childless couple in their thirties. They rented a broken-down adobe house and avoided paying rent by doing repairs. I met them through a blunder. I asked their yardman what he got paid for cutting the grass. "He" turned out to be Paula.

Wide-shouldered and small-breasted—superficially manly in appearance—Paula maneuvered the mower with the ease of long practice. Her hands were callused, nails bitten short. Hers is not the kind of beauty you recognize just by looking. You have to hold her in your arms and feel the muscles moving beneath her skin. Don't misunderstand, we were never lovers, but there were times when I held her and understood her beauty.

She shut the mower's engine in order to hear me. I saw my mistake then, but I pretended not to be surprised and calmly asked what she was paid.

"I get to sleep with the fella who lives here," she told me—an old joke, but we both laughed. By way of apology, I asked her and Eugene to dinner, and we quickly became friends.

Paula and I were both chronic early risers. She fell into the habit of dropping by while Eugene slept. I couldn't explain to friends what it was about her that made me look forward to those mornings. I hesitate to describe it now. She was an intelligent woman who thought and acted in a manner unlike anyone else I'd known. Despite that, I felt, almost from the beginning, as if I'd spent my whole life with her, although her life was as different from mine as dust is from coffee.

Our first important talk came late that summer, a brilliant morning after a night of rain. She propped her bare feet against my drop-leaf table and rocked back in her chair, a cup of coffee held with both hands, balanced in her lap. Sunlight from the slatted window over the kitchen sink fell across her hair. I stood at the kitchen counter, filling my cup. The smell of coffee permeated the room.

"You're the same height as my father," she said abruptly. Saying this embarrassed her, and she continued as if to justify having begun. "My father raised me by himself. We moved around a lot. He kept us moving."

I sat across from her and listened as a story emerged, staring all the while at her feet rising above the oak plane of the table, the feminine curve of her soles. I recall wondering why I hadn't noticed before the incredible beauty of her naked feet. How was that possible?

Paula's father, an itinerant salesman, once managed a trailer court in Apache Junction, Arizona, and set traps for the women who lived there. He and Paula kept up the miniature yards and accepted midday iced teas or lemonades from women home alone. Often, as they were about to leave a trailer, Paula's father would drop his wallet on a chair or beneath the kitchen table. When a woman sought him out and returned the wallet without taking the crumpled twenty he'd left inside, his immense gratitude would somehow make her beholden to him and he would seduce her. The others, the thieves, he also courted, making use of their guilt.

"He thought the trap was a good test of character," Paula said. "Though I don't know whether he preferred the women who took the money or those who returned it."

"He seduced them all?" I asked her.

"It seemed that way," she said with a mixture of both shame and pride. "There was one who mailed the wallet to him in a manila envelope. And another who had her husband return it. He didn't mess with them."

The intimacy of the story seemed to demand a reply. I shifted in my chair to avoid staring at her feet, reminding myself that Eugene slept just three houses away—the thick and dulling sleep of the unemployed. Thinking of him made me feel guilty. "Have I ever mentioned my ex-wife?" I asked her.

Paula said I hadn't.

I told her about how we'd met and what she'd said about love. "Sometimes I think she wanted children," I said, "although she always denied it. She was older than I was and a philosophy major, so I wanted to give her credit for deep thoughts. But all that about the products of love—kids are the obvious products of love, aren't they?"

Paula frowned at this. "Children are the product of screwing." She shook her head derisively. "And careless screwing, at that."

The Products of Love

"I guess I never did figure out what she meant," I admitted. "It seemed like a test I was constantly failing. Until finally our marriage failed. Your father's trap—his test—reminded me."

Paula let her chair settle against the floor and crossed her muscular arms. "Marriages are strange. Mine's strange. Can you tell? Does it show?"

"No," I said. "You and Eugene seem happy."

"I didn't say we weren't happy." She paused, as if wondering whether to continue. I put on another pot of coffee. She leaned back in the chair once more and began the story of her romance with Eugene.

They met in Colorado, a town north of Denver. Eugene taught mathematics at the high school where Paula cut the grass and raked litter. During his first month at the school, he called her into his classroom to complain that she had neither cleaned the blackboards nor swept the floor. She didn't tell him that she stood outside his window in order to trim the hedge that grew beneath it. Instead she retrieved a bucket, mop, and cloth from the storage room she shared with the custodian. While Eugene graded papers at his desk, Paula silently washed the blackboards and mopped the floor. She cleaned the room as a means of testing him.

A week later, he called her in again. "You manipulated me," he said to her flatly. "You let me behave badly."

Paula smiled at this, admiring him for turning the tables. "You're right," she said. "I apologize for mopping your floor."

Each afternoon that week, she made a point of stopping by. He made a point of waiting.

Wearing a white dress but carrying a bucket and sponge, she appeared one evening at the front door of his apartment. "I'm here to manipulate you again," she told him. She had to be persistent. A year passed before they became lovers, another five before he proposed. She had never worked so long and hard for anything, and success left her mildly deflated.

As long as she had remained the yardwoman at the high school, Eugene wouldn't marry her. He never said this openly, but he circled job descriptions in the classifieds and offered to borrow money from his parents to help her start a business.

Paula found work with a construction company, but her employment was erratic. She tried selling clothing for a few days. She considered managing a 7-Eleven. Finally, she landed a good job with the state on a road crew. The wedding quickly followed.

Mildly deflated: at times she thought of other men. Unable to sleep, sitting in her nightgown at the kitchen table, she recalled an artist in Santa Fe who had asked to photograph her, then dressed her in secondhand clothes and had her pose in a filthy alley. Afterward, he had shown such kindness to her body, a sort of tenderness she could only have guessed existed. She thought of him, then woke her husband, her fingertips at his ribs, his hips. Was this a vicarious form of adultery?

Even when it was solely Eugene who aroused her, how could she know it wasn't due to the way he carried his shoulders or lifted his chin, reminding her of some man she'd loved as a girl? She knew men had loved her for the woman they imagined. Later, when they saw her clearly, they would either leave her or continue to love her anyway. Paula had long ago separated the real Eugene from the man she imagined, but now she wondered whether she could separate real desire from imagined desire, separate real love from the tricks of memory.

Of course, Paula didn't tell me all of this that first morning. It came out in pieces, like a child's elaborate toy. It's taken concentration, and some guesswork, to assemble the parts.

* * *

The Products of Love

The road crew was widening a canyon two-lane into a freeway. The job required blasting. An enormous drill, held by two men, skewered rust-colored rock. Traffic in both directions was halted while engineers placed dynamite in the holes. The percussion echoed through the canyon. Boulders tumbled across the road and into the swift water. Caterpillars scooped up the mass of collapsed stone. Paula worked alongside other men and women, shoveling and sweeping, clearing the way for traffic backed a mile in either direction.

While she worked in the canyon, Paula had disturbing dreams, which she related in great detail to Eugene—and later to me. An example: Engineers place too many sticks of dynamite into the routed holes. Paula begins running. The whole of the canyon shudders with the explosion. She gallops past miles of stalled cars, while the canyon collapses behind her in a rush of dust and mayhem.

"Dream of me," Eugene told her when she recounted the nightmares in the bedroom of their little house in Colorado. He pressed his body against her, kissed her cheek. "You're so hot." He rocked his forehead, back and forth, against her neck. "My sweaty baby," he whispered, running his hand over her chest. "My working woman."

"Working woman work now," she said, opening her night-gown, crawling on top of him. "Working woman earn her keep."

Early June—ten months into their marriage—the weather abruptly turned. Two days before, there had been an inch of snow, but all at once the narrow canyon grew hot. Melting snow made the river rise and turn muddy brown. Paula's lungs suddenly shrank, making her pant, denying her breath. Minutes before the first blast, she found her supervisor and quit. A good state job, decent pay and benefits—Eugene called it a job with a future—but she'd had enough. Her supervisor, a kind man, gray sideburns showing beneath his fluorescent hard hat, nodded sadly at Paula, his lips pursed to indicate compassion.

Seeing no point in going home, Paula lit out in her truck, heading west across Colorado.

When she reached this point in her story, I remember saying, "You left Eugene?"

Paula nodded. "Without a word."

I'd invited them both to dinner, but Paula was called in to work at the last minute. She waitressed at a nearby steakhouse. Eugene came alone and brought Mexican beer. He had East Coast looks, if there is such a thing—dark hair but a light complexion, the rumpled, sinewy type. He'd been educated at private schools in Connecticut, and the way he slouched handsomely in a chair seemed practiced.

I made enchiladas and green chili. I enjoy cooking, but most of my friends are vegetarians. That's one of the reasons I first liked Paula and Eugene—they were unapologetic meat eaters.

"Paula's told you about us, right?" Eugene said.

"A little," I admitted. We'd finished eating but remained at the table to drink. "She said the two of you were separated for a while."

"Separated?"

"That's my word, really."

"She left me is what happened. She ran away. I still don't know what went on, exactly, during that time." He hesitated, glancing at me as if I might fill in the missing parts. When I said nothing, he finished his beer and helped himself to another.

"Women are mysterious," he said. "Not men. Men are simple, you know? Men are like cars: once you understand the mechanics of them, they're simple. But women . . . women are like the ocean. You following me?"

"We're Chevys," I said. "They're the Mediterranean."

"You think you understand her, but there's no end to her. Do you know that the Pacific is deeper than Everest is high?"

Eventually, I coaxed him into telling his side of the story.

When Paula didn't return from work, Eugene called her supervisor and heard that she'd quit and driven her truck west—the opposite direction of their home. Eugene immediately blamed himself, thinking she must have heard about Willa Abrams. He fetched the road atlas from the kitchen pantry and traced his finger along the route Paula had taken. He drank gin in the big reclining chair his mother had given them as a wedding gift, the phone on the table beside him.

Eugene had long loved Willa Abrams. A married woman. Two daughters, a Labrador, a ninety-thousand-dollar mortgage, a swimming pool. Willa and Philip Abrams had married in the early sixties on Eugene's tenth birthday, a coincidence that caused him considerable pain. He'd slept with Willa during the years he dated Paula, cutting it off only after he and Paula became engaged. During their ten months of marriage, he'd seen Willa secretly, although—Eugene was adamant about this—they no longer made love.

He related an episode with Willa that took place early on, before he and Paula were lovers. To Willa, he'd said, "I'm testing you." Paula had told him about her father's trap.

Willa laughed contemptuously. "The teacher must give all his girls tests," she said. She pointed at him with her wine glass, which was filled with Scotch and ice—they'd both had a lot to drink—and said, "Let me have it. What is my test?"

"*This* is your test. Right now," he explained. "How you behave."

She nodded in mock seriousness. A sleek and handsome

woman with arching brows and nostrils, she'd recently turned forty and wore a new hairstyle, dyeing all but a few strands of the gray. "How I behave," she muttered. She set her drink on the coffee table, then leapt onto the couch and began running in place on the cushions. She lifted her skirt and made animal noises, naming them.

"The donkey," she yelled. "Hee-haw! Hee-haw! The rooster. Cockadoodle-doo!" She worked her legs so feverishly that Eugene could not resist and began laughing.

When she finally fell to her knees beside him, she said, "Now you may tell the janitor that I behaved like an animal—several animals." She was panting and lay her head against his leg. "Did I pass the test?" she asked him.

"Maybe," he told her. "If I grade on a curve."

She lifted her head and moved close to his face. "The janitor" —she always referred to Paula as "the janitor" and Eugene no longer corrected her—"is another symbol in your dreamily self-destructive motif—"

"Of which you were the first element," he quickly added.

"Screw you," Willa said calmly. "Don't interrupt me."

"Paula doesn't mind when I interrupt."

"Then screw the both of you."

She finished her drink and spat ice cubes into his lap. "Marry the janitor for all I care. Let her have your idiot children. That'll be the result of your love—tiny drooling idiots."

All of Eugene's stories about Willa included this sort of nastiness, but they were told with real longing. He didn't realize that they cast her in a bad light.

The night that Paula left him, Eugene slept in the chair beside the phone and woke there the following morning, groggy but not as badly hung over as he would have guessed. However, he had wet his pants. Seeing this, he burst into tears.

"I cried like a child," he told me. "I was miserable."

I couldn't think of a way to respond, which added to the embarrassment of his confession. Finally, I said, "When my wife left, I drank and acted like a moron. We had an old refrigerator that wasn't keeping my beer cold. I hacked at the ice around the freezer so the door would close tightly. I used an ice pick and it had the predictable result. Freon sprayed across the room. The floor became slick with it."

We laughed, a masculine sort of chortle. "What'd you do then?" Eugene wanted to know.

"I took off my shoes and slid across the room in my socks, sloshing my beer everywhere." We roared at this. "I turned the stereo up as high as it would go and skated on my kitchen floor."

It had been the most pathetic night of my life. Eugene and I became nearly hysterical, laughing at our manly displays of weakness.

A young Mexican family lives in the house directly behind mine. They own a late model Corvette, which they rescued from a wrecking yard and repaired on their own, although it doesn't yet run. For years the car has had its gray primer paint, but they have never gotten around to (or can't afford) the final coat of color. Nevertheless, the car is a source of pride. They wash it every Saturday afternoon. Their children eat cantaloupe and watch. Friends drop by to help.

I'd been a regular washer of the Corvette for months and convinced Eugene and Paula to join. Eugene knew a little about cars and tried to help with the repair. "It needs a whole new engine," he told me confidentially. "It'll never run otherwise." This news discouraged him, but Paula and I continued to scrub the car weekly.

Several months passed before Paula confided what happened

after she ran away. She never once mentioned Willa Abrams. I came to understand that she knew nothing about Eugene's love for another woman. She never considered it possible. Even now, I'm the only one who knows the whole story.

As you've already guessed, I fell in love with Paula. That was my part of the story, and I tried to keep it secret. I never had an affair while I was married, and I never slept with a married woman after my divorce. The desire I felt for Paula contradicted the way I wanted to live.

I suppose I should have stopped seeing her altogether, but all we did was talk. Besides, the story was not finished, and I wanted to have all the pieces. This may sound strange, but I'd begun taking notes, filling in what was left unsaid. My job permitted me to work at home, illustrating and editing computer manuals. Every day I'd alternate between computer jargon and the story of Paula and Eugene. Paula's voice, low and feminine, would return to me throughout the day. I carried her with me the way her hair carried the scent of the sun.

One day after washing the Corvette, she and I went to my kitchen to make sandwiches for everyone. While we fried bacon and sliced tomatoes, I persuaded her to resume the story.

As soon as her pickup began moving down the canyon road, Paula was able to breathe again. She flew past the waiting line of eastbound cars. When the explosion came, she was miles away, the sound nothing more than hands clapping. Hours later she pulled her truck into a gas station, now in Colorado flatland, the temperature reading ninety-two degrees. Paula had grown up in the desert. Hot weather could be as oppressive to her as certain old songs. The gas attendant suggested Telluride—nine thousand feet and a pretty place. People were going there that weekend to hear bluegrass, a kind of music Paula didn't like, but she headed in that direction.

Her arrival in Telluride corresponded with the breakdown of the dishwashing machine in The Nugget Bar and Grill. She found herself working before she had a place to stay. "Keep your butt moving," the owner told her. "There's always something that needs to be done."

"The guy's a jerk," the cook said to Paula after the owner left. "A ski-head. Born into money, then married more money. All he knows is skiing and money." The cook's name was Cyrano Cook. He went by Cook. "I ought to do *anything* else," he said, "but cooking's all I'm good at." Under his white apron, he wore a spaghetti-strap T-shirt, which revealed big shoulders and muscled arms tattooed with several Navy insignia.

"Were you a cook in the Navy?" Paula asked him.

"Hell no," he said. "I was Joe Swabby—you know, 'Swab them decks.' Try to get a job around here doing *that*."

The lone waitress, Stevie, was in her twenties and barked her orders at Cook, then thanked him when she picked up the prepared plates.

"I force her to say thanks," Cook confessed. "Makes my job nicer that way." Then he added, "She's Kirk's girl."

Kirk was the bartender. He stayed out of the kitchen. Paula saw him only when she carried a tray of glasses to the front—a conventionally handsome man who had a bartender's ingratiating smile. "The machine never did this," he said, smiling, referring to Paula's delivery of the glasses. The second time she brought him a tray, he said it again, which made Paula think he was nervous around her. She found this endearing.

After closing, Paula stayed to help Kirk and Stevie clean. Kirk made a pitcher of margaritas and put reggae on the stereo. When Paula revealed that she didn't have a place to stay, they offered to rent her a room. They owned a condominium by the river and leased the room to skiers during the season. "You'd have to move out after summer," Stevie told her. "We charge skiers a lot more." Paula assured them that she wouldn't be in the same straits by then.

"This is a great place to live," Kirk told her. They had left by the back door, passed through the alley, and out onto the sloping mountain street. The condo was within walking distance, and Paula trailed them home. "Movie stars come here on vacation," Kirk said. "We saw Jane Fonda last month."

"We think it was Jane Fonda," Stevie said.

"I used to live in Malibu," Kirk continued, "and I'd see Mary Tyler Moore in the grocery store all the time. Once I was in line with Linda Ronstadt."

"I guess everybody has to eat," Paula offered.

Her room was small but with a view of the San Miguel River. She fell quickly to sleep, but woke up with a start an hour before dawn, realizing that she had left her truck on the street near the Nugget. She dressed quickly in the same clothes she'd worn to work that morning—the only clothes she had with her—and tiptoed outside.

Cold and wet, the night air pressed against her face as she trotted up the sidewalk. She wondered whether Eugene had called the police to report her missing. This was the first time she'd permitted herself to think of him, and it caused a deep pain in her chest. The peaks of the San Juans loomed over Telluride. Above the mountains floated a half moon. In storefront windows, her skin shone blue.

The truck rested peacefully against the curb. Paula considered driving across the state and returning home. Instead, she pushed in the clutch and let the truck coast down the asphalt to the condominium.

"In one day, I quit my job, left home, moved across the state, got a new job, new friends, and a new place to live," Paula said. "It was the busiest day of my life."

"You're an amazing woman," I told her.

She shook her head. "My father once had and quit four jobs in three different towns within twenty-four hours. To top it off, he stole something from each place."

"Where was your mother when all of this went on?"

"Dead. Pneumonia. My father claims she was always frail." As if to prove her own heartiness, Paula lifted my ficus tree and moved it next to the window. "Needs all the light it can get," she explained. "I've been meaning to do that for months."

I thanked her. She looked at me expectantly, as if I might offer more. She said, "In some ways, leaving Eugene was easy. It's the kind of thing I'm capable of doing."

That was the first moment I had the courage to think she might love me, too.

The nights Paula did not work, the three of us went to the movies. Then Eugene started graduate school, and Paula and I went out alone. We pretended otherwise, but we were relieved to be without him. More and more, I grew confident that she loved me. This became the only subject matter that was taboo. We made our time together safe by including Eugene even when he was absent, discussing whether he would have enjoyed the film, the meal, the wash of stars across the heavens.

I know this sounds corny, but our love had become a source of light, a glow that illuminated the world around us. Walking together one night, I actually saw it—light circled our bodies and fell to the sidewalk at our feet, light that emanated from our hearts and shone through our flimsy skin.

However, we didn't hold hands while we walked. Once we acknowledged it, our love would cast a shadow over Paula's marriage, over my friendship with Eugene. It would spoil the reconciliation whose story I was still attempting to construct. We protected the light by letting our love go unrecognized. We lived our lie happily.

One night Eugene revealed that Paula had decided to set me up with a waitress at the restaurant. "Beautiful woman," Eugene said. "I told her to do it, but she changed her mind. Seems she can't locate anybody good enough for you."

I smiled along with Eugene and quickly changed the subject, overjoyed that Paula could not find it in herself to introduce me to another woman.

Until he started graduate school, Eugene and I watched a lot of television. Baseball, especially, but other sports, too. We talked while we watched, conversations interrupted by cheers for good plays. Once he asked me if he was in the way, wondering whether I was seeing a woman. I told him no. It wasn't until I lay in bed that night that I realized he was trying to feel jealous. But Eugene was no more capable of believing that Paula might love me than she was able to imagine his loving Willa.

He told me that Willa could not understand why, once Paula was out of the way, he would not sleep with her. The exchange I'm about to relate took place in the living room of Eugene and Paula's rented house two days after Paula disappeared. The afternoon sun shone through the windows, which were large and square. The furniture, unmatched pieces Paula had purchased at yard sales, were made of laminated wood and foam-rubber cushions. Eugene preferred the big chair his mother had given them. I picture him in that chair as the conversation began.

"I just can't," Eugene told Willa, his head falling back against the soft headrest. "That's what got me into all this trouble in the first place." They were talking about making love, but he was referring more generally to their love.

"What trouble?" Willa insisted. From what I know of her, I would guess the uncomfortable couch offended her sensibility as well as her body, embodying her vision of Paula—trashy, second-rate, cheap.

"My wife has left me," Eugene went on. "You may see that as a wonderful thing, but I don't."

"Did she ever go to school for any purpose but to mow the grass?" Willa asked, stretching out now on the offensive couch.

"She's smarter than you think." Eugene jumped from his chair and began pacing about the room. "She may even be smarter than I am. She just doesn't have much education."

"A magpie is smarter than you. Magpies at least seek out entertainment and take it without feeling guilty."

"Say what you want." He leaned against the wall with his arm and elbow. "You happen to be intelligent *and* well educated. Paula is every bit as smart as you, but she never finished high school. She ran away."

"It's a habit then, this running off?" Seeing that he would not respond, she said, "Oh, that poor, poor, poor child. The waif. The darling. If only I could find the poor thing and wrench her neck."

"She'd knock you silly." He turned and faced her, a bit of drama in his eyes. "Don't kid yourself. She's worked all her life. I've seen her carry—"

"Thank you, thank you for this informative aside. I'll take care to shoot the bitch from long distance. Please shut up about her."

"My wife is missing, Willa. What would you like me to talk about?"

"Missing?" She laughed at him. "She's not missing. You think someone kidnapped her?"

"All right, all right."

"The janitor dumped you like yesterday's garbage," she said.

"She was never a janitor. Don't call her that." He began pacing again, his hands shoved deep inside his pockets. His mind's peculiar logic frightened him: the more he defended Paula, the more aware he became of his abiding desire for Willa. "I think you should go. I want you to go now."

"I don't feel like going."

Eugene walked into the bathroom and locked the door. Paula had left a paperback by the toilet and he began reading. Willa cursed him loudly. She hurled record albums against the walls. The crashes lent to his act a feeling of righteousness. He read Louis L'Amour and waited for Willa to tire and go home.

Near closing time, Paula's third night on the job, a stranger appeared, a short man with curly blond hair, rapping gently at the rear of the Nugget. Paula removed her hands from the soapy water, and stepped to the screen door.

In the harsh light of the back alley, the man's milk-white face shone as clear as a child's. When he spoke, his voice was soft and friendly. "Girl named Stevie Welsh work here?"

"Yeah," Paula said. "You need to go around front."

The man squinted and shook his head. "Could you ask her to come back here for a moment?"

Before Paula could reply, Cook yelled, "No! We're working."

Paula shrugged, as if in apology, and stepped away. Later she saw him at the bar. "He found you," Paula said. Stevie had come into the kitchen for an order. She nodded, but offered nothing.

Cleaning up that night was an especially drunken affair. Paula wanted to ask Stevie about the mysterious man but thought she shouldn't in front of Kirk. She drank so many piña coladas she became emotional. "I *have* to do something with my life," she exclaimed suddenly.

"You are doing something," Kirk told her. "You're living here. Who wouldn't want to live here?" He pinched her bottom and forced her to dance with him, which eventually cheered her.

"You're my family now," she said, insisting on dancing with Stevie after Kirk. "We're sisters, me and you."

"We're loaded," Stevie corrected her.

Stevie declined a second dance. She spent a lot of time in the bathroom. When Paula looked in on her, she was standing in front of the mirror touching her face. "Wrinkles," she explained.

The cold night air sobered them. They had taken only a few steps into the alley when Stevie said, "I was afraid you'd still be here."

Only then did Paula see the man, the strange man. He wasn't all that big, and his face was gentle, pale. He said to Stevie, "It's a matter of integrity."

Paula could tell he'd had nothing to drink, which made her worry. Who spent all evening in a bar without drinking?

But Stevie threw her arms around him, twisting back and forth in his embrace. When she told Kirk and Paula to go on home, she was smiling. She even teased them about warming up the bed for her.

Kirk should have been upset, but when Stevie winked at him, he returned it and took Paula's arm. He grabbed playfully at her as they headed toward the river.

Drunk as Paula was, they might even have gotten into bed together, but Kirk had forgotten his keys. No one had made a copy for Paula yet. They had to hurry back and catch Stevie.

When they got back, not more than twenty minutes from the time they left, they found Stevie dead.

Paula screamed.

They happened upon her in the alley, her body draped over the concrete stoop of the Nugget.

Kirk said, "How do you figure?" More than a minute passed before he began to cry and slumped to his knees, falling against the greasy screen door.

Stevie's throat had a long, ragged tear. Blood covered her face and drenched her hair, as if she'd been lifted by the feet to drain like a butchered animal. The police nóted that Stevie still had her wallet and keys. She had not been raped. One said, "A shame the kind of people these concerts drag in." Paula told him music had nothing to do with it, but Kirk got most of the attention. He didn't say much about the stranger who had murdered his girlfriend, but he took a good photograph and it ran in the local papers.

Paula never missed an hour of work, which Cook found cold-blooded. "What could I have done?" she asked me. "I didn't know a soul outside the Nugget." The owner filled in as waiter the first night, then traded jobs with Paula. Before another week passed, the dishwasher had been repaired and Paula had Stevie's old job. Cook remained distant with Paula the remainder of her time in Telluride.

"Had he been in love with Stevie?" I asked.

"I don't think so."

"Were you in love with him?"

"With Cook? Are you joking?"

"Well?"

"I can't explain his behavior. Or mine," she said. Then she added, "It's lousy when someone you like thinks you're a bad person."

This conversation, I recall now, took place on my patio one cloudy morning. The air was charged with the coming heat but wasn't yet hot. Paula, barefoot as always, rested her feet on my picnic table, heel and sole facing me, blackened with dirt, her chair rocking back and forth on its rear legs.

During the second year I knew Paula and Eugene, we had an adventure together. We spent the day in Mexico, in a border town not far from here, shopping and eating.

Eugene tried out his college Spanish in an increasingly aggressive manner. By evening, he was bartering for trinkets that he had no intention of buying. "I've been too shy with the neighbors," he said expansively. "I figured they'd know more English than I would Spanish, but it's all come back."

We'd begun drinking at lunch and stopped various times to snack and have another beer. Paula bought a leather jacket—Eugene bargaining for twenty minutes in order to save two dollars. After dark, she slipped it on. It was November and the night was cool. I purchased a large wooden mask. I have a collection of primitive masks, and this was a find—the head of a coyote in whose open mouth is a fierce-looking crow, and in the bird's mouth is a snake, whose open mouth reveals the mouth of the wearer.

I wanted to sober up before the drive home. We found a bar near the border where Eugene and Paula continued to drink. A woman at another table began staring at me. She was roughly my age, a bit heavy through the middle, but attractive and familiar, although I couldn't place her. Eventually, she left her friends and came to our table. She put her hand on my shoulder. "Don't you remember me?" she said.

"Please join us," I said.

Paula introduced herself, saving me the embarrassment of asking the woman's name. "I was his wife's best friend way back when," Julia Mills said. "We were all close." She took my hand from the table and patted it, then pressed it between her palms.

We reminisced for a while. Julia had married twice and was twice divorced. She had not heard from my wife in a long time. I told her what I knew.

"You took it hard," she said to me.

"I suppose I did," I said, "but that was a million years ago." By the time I felt sober enough to drive, she had told her friends she'd catch a ride with us.

The sky was cloudless, cold and dark. I switched on the heater and we hunched together, all four of us in the front seat, as the rear was filled with computer manuals and the mask. Pressed against the passenger window, Eugene fell asleep and began to snore.

Paula said, "When I first met him, he didn't snore."

Julia commiserated. "Both my husbands snored." Then she slapped my knee. "You don't snore, though. You're the only grown man I know who doesn't snore."

"What makes you so sure?" I asked her.

She answered by speaking to Paula. "His wife and I used to tiptoe in while he was asleep and trim his hair. He had long, long hair back then. The worst split ends you've ever seen. And he never snored a bit."

"I wasn't asleep," I told her.

"Sometimes you were," she insisted.

Julia and Paula talked for the remainder of the drive, but an ache had begun in my chest and I kept quiet. I had forgotten that dark bedroom, the flannel sheets that had been a wedding gift, the sounds of young women trying to be silent as they approached me, their fingers in my hair, the scissors opening and closing so close to my ear, the music of restrained female laughter.

Eugene revived himself at the trip's end. We decided to have another drink in my kitchen. Although they lived just three houses away, Paula and Eugene spent the night in the guest bedroom. Julia slept with me. "I always had a crush on you," she confessed.

That morning, Paula entered the bathroom and found me on my knees before the toilet. She wore only a T-shirt but stretched it with her hand to cover herself. I was naked, my elbows on the porcelain, waiting for the upheaval that was not to come.

"Can I do anything?" she asked, then knelt beside me and rested her hand on my back.

"I don't like being seen like this," I said and turned my head, as if not seeing her were the same as not being seen.

While I stared into the bowl, her hair touched my shoulders and her lips—unmistakably her lips—brushed across my back. Then she rose and left the room.

That was the only time Paula kissed me.

As it turned out, Julia was just in town for the weekend. She hadn't lived in the desert in fifteen years. Sometimes she calls, but we haven't seen each other since that night.

A month after Stevie's death, Kirk still hadn't returned to the bar. All he seemed capable of doing was cooking. Paula came home at two in the morning to veal in wine sauce or chicken cooked in cognac. The meals were excessive and badly done— the meat overcooked, the sauces too sweet. But Paula supposed it was something like therapy for him. She ate whatever he prepared.

One night after burnt lamb chops and a viscous Greek salad, Kirk appeared at her bedroom door wearing pajamas, a plaid long-sleeved shirt and matching pants. "Would you mind?" he said. "I'm not getting any rest. I need to sleep." Then he added, "You've been so good to me."

He wanted Paula to talk while he lay with his eyes closed and drifted. The first night, Paula told him the plot of a sitcom she'd seen. Talking and sleeping was all they did for several nights, but Paula knew it was the kind of situation where one thing would lead to another.

She let it happen. Soon Kirk began acting toward her as he had toward Stevie, whom, Paula found out later, he'd known only three weeks before they pooled their money to buy the condo.

Paula moved into Stevie's bed, shared it with Stevie's boyfriend, and paid for it by working at Stevie's job. She even wore Stevie's old uniform and some of her clothes. She had hardly known Stevie before she was killed, but she was getting to know her better all the time.

One of the first things she realized was that Kirk was a lot more attractive when he was someone else's boyfriend. He had trouble following conversations. At times he smiled or winked or pinched her butt, which had a certain boyish charm, but she discovered that it meant he hadn't understood her, didn't have a clue as to what she was talking about. All the flirting things— the way he licked his lips or pinched her or lifted her blouse and wiggled a finger in her belly button—were repeated so often that she started seeing them as his own little short list of personality.

Stevie's job fared better than her boyfriend. When winter came, skiers filled the bar nightly. A second waitress was hired. Kirk went back to bartending, and Paula's former room was rented for the whole season to a kid from New Jersey whose father owned a tool company.

Cook became especially disdainful of Paula when he heard that she and Kirk were lovers. "You landed on your feet," he said to her.

"I'm not the one who was thrown," she replied. "Kirk was thrown. I just stumbled into the middle of it."

"And you sure made the most of it."

"You don't know the first thing about me." She sounded angry but was more hurt than mad. For whatever reason, Cook had become her touchstone in this new place. Impulsively, she told him about Eugene, how she had left her husband without a word. "You are now the only person I've told."

"I guess that explains something," Cook said. "I don't see how, but I guess it does."

"Why are you so mad at me?"

"Who said I was? If I was, I won't be, all right?"

That was the end of the conversation. That night at home, Cook phoned information for the number of Eugene Loroun. He never told Paula this, and he didn't dial Eugene's number that night. Eugene said the call came in March. They talked for a long time before Cook revealed the whereabouts of Eugene's wife.

I sometimes find myself thinking about the months that passed between the point when Cook obtained Eugene's number and the day he called. What a treasure he had, valuable only as long as he refused to spend it.

"It was a peculiar life, living with a man I didn't love or have any kind of feelings for, not having friends except Cook, who would still be a bastard half the time, but it had become my life anyway. I wasn't thinking, 'This is what I'm doing until my real life starts up again.' It was my real life." Paula had come to my house in a brand-new bathing suit. I have no pool and she made no mention of swimming or even sitting in the yard and sunning. She carried a small purse with a long strap looped around her bare shoulder.

I made eggs. This was near the end, shortly before she and Eugene moved away. Outside, beyond my yard, the neighbors hauled out buckets of soapy water to wash their stationary car, but on this day neither of us considered helping. Paula, in her pink one-piece, rocked on the back legs of a kitchen chair—she never sat still—and talked about the night Eugene appeared at the bar.

He was alone at a table watching her. When she approached, he said, "I'll have a gin and tonic." Then he added, "It's good to see you." He claimed that he had tracked her all over the state.

Paula was moved by the story of his search. She felt the familiar combination of tenderness and fear that comes with love. But the fear was darker. Not the apprehension that usually accompanies strong feeling, but some larger fear.

Eugene drank his gin and talked about the high school and their neighbors, all that had happened while she'd been away. He did not ask about her motives for leaving. She understood that he was giving her the opportunity to come back.

But her anxiety grew, despite the friendly talk. Much later she would figure out the nature of the fear. At the time, all she could do was act on it.

She went into the back and took off her apron. "See you," she said to Cook and slipped out the back door. In another hour she was on the highway, following the Dolores River west. She angled across New Mexico and then hurtled through the White Mountains of Arizona. As it was March and still cold in the high altitudes, she decided to return to the desert. Which is how she wound up here.

"I didn't figure it out for a long time," Paula told me. She scooted her chair away from the table, close to mine, and crossed her legs. Her bathing suit was the pink of my roses. "I was happy to see Eugene, but this fear . . ." She looked at my face several moments, not into my eyes but all around my face. Through the open windows, phrases of Spanish drifted in. "There aren't many things I'm afraid of," she said.

"What was it?" I asked.

She shook her head and stood, suddenly angry with me. "There I was in Stevie's old life and damned if someone from my past hadn't tracked me down. Don't you see?" She became exasperated. "Aren't you going to say anything?"

"How did the two of you finally get back together?" It was the wrong thing to say. She charged out of my house, leaving her purse.

The one lie—if you do not count silence as a lie—that Eugene had told Paula was that he had tracked her down. Cook had called him. But there had been someone tracking her.

"Willa hired a detective," Eugene explained. "She thought once I saw Paula again I'd become enraged. She thought I was making Paula out to be larger than life."

The detective failed to locate Paula, but months later he did manage to find Eugene. "Willa called me this morning, out of the blue," Eugene told me. "Same old Willa. Says as soon as her daughters are in college, she'll leave Phil. I hate that name, Phil. I hate proper names that are verbs."

"What did you say to her?" I asked.

"I told her we were through." He threw his hands up, as if in resignation. "There's no percentage in the past," he said sadly.

I asked him then how he'd caught up with Paula after she left the Nugget. He didn't respond directly. "Willa used to say awful things about Phil. She did impersonations."

"I've never mentioned Willa to your wife," I said.

"I know that," Eugene snapped. "No one's accusing you of anything."

I left the room to pour myself a drink and let him cool off. He caught up with me. "Make me one, too," he said. I gave him my bourbon and he downed it. "When I was a school teacher I knew who I was. I had Paula, I had a job I liked, I more or less had Willa." He held the glass over his mouth to let the last drops fall on his tongue. "Does Paula make fun of me? Is that what you two do?"

"No," I said. "She thinks the world of you."

His smile was ironic. "The world's gone to hell lately, hasn't it?"

After another drink, he resumed the story.

When Paula didn't return from the back of the bar, Eugene guessed what had happened. Telluride is a box canyon. There is only one road out. He drove to the edge of town, thinking he'd have a while to wait, believing that Paula would pack some clothes, but she had merely run to her truck and taken off. If she hadn't gotten into the habit of leaving the pickup at the condominium and walking to work, he would have missed her altogether.

He followed her for hours, keeping his distance. When she finally pulled into the Desert Aire Motel, he waited in his idling car, trying to decide what to do. The car's engine sputtered and died—he'd run the tank completely dry. He took this to be a sign.

He left his car by the side of the road and walked to the room he'd seen Paula enter. He knocked gently.

Telling me about this moment, Eugene became shy. "She didn't seem surprised," he said. "She put her arms around me and took me inside."

Paula was more generous with details. "For the last hour of the drive, I'd regretted leaving him. But it was done, and I didn't see any way to undo it. I had just taken off my shoes when I heard the knocking. I thought, 'That would be Eugene. He's tracked me down again.' And there he was."

He had stood in the doorway with his hands clasped together on top of his head, eyes red from the long drive, hair stiff from the wind. The first thing she did was touch his flannel shirt. One of the buttons had come undone and she buttoned it.

"I'm tired," he told her.

She nodded and said, "It was a long drive." They embraced.

This embrace should end the story. They found a house on my street. Paula got a job. Eugene eventually received a graduate degree in high-school administration. But it's the embrace that shows the lovers together again, the embrace that provides the story with a happy ending.

However, Eugene left Paula after finishing his degree. His leave-taking was not dramatic. He consulted a lawyer, an agreement was reached.

The day he drove away, I broke the silence. "I love you," I told her. We were on the telephone. She hadn't come to my house in weeks, wouldn't open her door to me. "This clears the way for us, don't you see? Before, it would have been so . . ."

"Inconvenient," she said.

"Come live with me."

"Not now," she told me. "Not like this."

"Why won't you?"

She said, "It's a matter of integrity."

A pain rocked my chest, as if I had been struck by a hammer. "I should have . . ."

"You should have moved. You should have made a move." The phone went dead.

I've come to understand that the light that had engulfed us was not love. Love permits the light, creates the light, but is not the light. We concealed our love to protect the light, much like throwing a blanket over a fire to conserve heat.

But there was more to it than that. Something Paula doesn't understand—I alone knew the whole story. The little misunderstandings they each clung to, the aberrations of logic, the lies, the failings of faith, the odd course their love had taken. I knew it all, and knowing paralyzed me.

Eugene lives in California and says Paula is somewhere in New Mexico. She's asked him not to tell me where. This is the ultimate product of our love: we're each alone, spread across the Southwest.

Maybe I should include Willa, too. She's still in Colorado with her husband and children and swimming pool, longing for Eugene. And I suppose my ex-wife should get her due. She's remained single all these years. At Christmas she sends me a card. The last one was from Moab, Utah. "I have a nice yard here," the card read, "room for tomato plants and a few stalks of corn. I refinished our old chairs. You remember those chairs?"

Love advances mysteriously. The wind remains invisible. We shudder in its wake. I understand now, finally, that love is more important than happiness.

The last time I spoke face-to-face with Paula was when she came by in her bathing suit. That evening, after supper, while Eugene readied himself to leave, I retrieved his wife's purse, which still rested on the kitchen chair.

"Must be new." Eugene had entered the room and took the little bag that dangled from my finger. He immediately opened it and thrust his hand inside. His expression quickly changed. "Oh, Paula," he said softly, as if she were standing beside him.

"What is it?" I asked, but he had already walked away. "Hold on," I said. "Have another beer."

He didn't reply but stopped at the door and revealed the contents of the purse: a single twenty-dollar bill.

He turned and stepped out into the dark. The pace he set was not fast but steady. His shoulders cut the night squarely. Before entering his house, he raised his arm as if to wave, but it was only to show me the purse a final time.

Imagining Spaniards

The summer Eddie Net turned fifteen, his Uncle Abe was paroled from Florence State Penitentiary and moved in with Eddie's family. He had served eleven years for armed robbery. "The war was hard on him," Eddie's father explained. While he and Abe had been overseas, their parents and little brother were killed in a fire. Abe's fiancée died of cancer. "Everybody he loved died while he was in Italy—everyone but me," said Eddie's father. "We used to claim the war saved us."

Unlike the rest of the family, Abe was tall, over six feet, although his shoulders and neck slumped forward. An athlete in his youth, he had quit school at fourteen to play professional baseball. When war broke out, he was pitching for the Asheville Tourists, a veteran minor leaguer and part-time apprentice carpenter. He had grown thin eating prison food and developed a facial tic—a half-wink of his right eye. A metal cafeteria tray hurled by an arsonist had broken his nose, causing it to angle sharply left. "A bridge with a detour," Abe liked to say. The year was 1969. He was fifty-three and found work running a pool hall in downtown Tucson for less than minimum wage.

Eddie and his friends played eight ball at the Silver Cue for free. In exchange for the games, Eddie helped Abe with the nightly cleanup. He swept cigarette butts and sprays of chalk from the wooden floor, and filled crates with empty pop bottles. The Silver Cue prohibited liquor, and players drank between games in their cars. By closing time, beer cans and wine bottles littered the parking lot. Eddie swept the debris into a pile with a pushbroom. He and Abe counted the cans as they tossed them into the trash bucket.

The final night of July, Eddie and Abe counted forty-seven cans—six short of the record. They lugged the garbage out back to the alley. A new dumpster shone white in the moon's glare, standing eight feet high with a little door like a mouth halfway up. They shoved the trash through the door.

Uncle Abe said, "This the stupidest garbage can I ever seen. A full growed man's got to get in there and shovel it out over his head."

Eddie explained that a truck with long handles scooped up the white dumpster, lifted it over the cab, and dumped it upside down into the truck bed.

Unable to imagine it, Abe laughed at first, perhaps thinking that Eddie was joking. Then he grew quiet, and they stepped back inside. While they loaded the Coke machine—their final chore—Abe offered to teach Eddie how to shoot combinations. When Eddie hesitated, Abe said, "Your pa won't mind."

They shot pool together through the night. Abe demonstrated the uses of spin, the angles of approaching a ball, the significance of touch. He emphasized the importance of the cue ball's placement after a made shot. "That's a good leave there," he said softly after Eddie made an easy shot. "But call the kiss next time. Some won't count it if you don't call the kiss. If we was playing for money, I wouldn't."

Eddie's father joined them at about three that morning. He appeared in his canvas jacket at the glass door, tapping lightly, as if there were nothing unusual in his son spending all night in a pool hall.

Eddie's father and uncle played a long game of straight pool. They hardly spoke. The movement of their cues, the shapes their bodies took as they bent over the table, the touch on their shots—these served in the place of words. Until this night, Eddie had found it impossible to see his father and Abe as brothers.

At one point Eddie's father said, "You're off your game."

Abe shrugged. His eye half-winked. "Happens."

Eddie's father seemed to know that this night was not the product of whim or carelessness. Abe had grown grimly serious. Eddie had not understood this until he watched his father and uncle shoot pool.

Shortly before dawn, Abe led them out to the alley. They sat on a concrete stoop. Abe rolled cigarettes, which he and Eddie's father smoked. Abe whistled "When Johnny Comes Marching Home." He tried to whistle smoke rings, a talent he had acquired in prison.

Minutes before the earliest light, a truck roared down the alley, stopping in front of them with a hydraulic hiss. The dumpster shone dazzling white in the glare of high beams as the truck extended its metal arms and edged forward, guiding those arms into their slots. The truck cradled the dumpster. The arms rose above the cab and over, emptying the garbage into the back.

Abe said, "Slam dunk." He pulled hard on his cigarette. "Need a degree these days to take out the trash," he added. A sardonic smile flickered across his face. His eye twitched.

Two nights later, Abe disappeared. He left a note that Eddie was not permitted to see for years. It said simply *Can't hack it.* The final weekend of the summer Abe held up a liquor store in Phoenix. He spent the last years of his life in prison.

A decade after the incident, the first night of his marriage to Jennifer Schacterly, Eddie related this story while they lay in their honeymoon bed. It was the first thing either had said after making love. He told her what he thought, that Abe discovered that the world was too changed for him to stay in it. Jennifer liked the story, but she couldn't see how Abe understood all that from an unfamiliar garbage dumpster.

Eddie sat up on the mattress, imitating the way Abe had sat in the alley, his knees doubled up almost to his chin. He described his uncle's sideburns that reached his jaw, the wrinkled mustard-colored shirt, his stained fingers wrapping tobacco in crisp white paper.

"You loved your uncle," Jennifer said, her voice sad and solicitous.

Eddie had loved his uncle, but that was not what he was trying to express. "Close your eyes," he said. He asked her to imagine ancient Spaniards who had just heard about the discovery of the New World. This, he believed, was the sensation his uncle experienced, except that for Abe the Old World no longer existed—there was this new world and nothing else.

Jennifer smiled and touched his bare chest. While imagining Spaniards, she fell asleep.

Eddie tried to sleep, too, but death had entered his honeymoon bed, turning his stomach, chilling his extremities, making the odor of their nuptial sex heavy and oppressive.

For more than a week, death made itself evident to him in the shallowness of every embrace, in the blandness of all food, in the moments after sex when Eddie knew the limitations of the body to speak for the heart.

After nine days, the darkness mysteriously lifted. Eddie again felt the joy of new love.

Years passed. Eddie recalled those nine dreary days rarely—occasionally while reading or sitting in a movie theater, once when he'd seen an exhibition of the paintings of van Gogh—and in each case he quickly dismissed the memory.

Not that he didn't think about death. His father had died during this time, and he heard of the deaths of two men he had known as boys. His mother called one night to say that a woman he had dated in high school died of AIDS. He thought about death when, while watching on television a colorized version of *Top Hat*, he learned that the film was being presented in memory of Fred Astaire—the announcement quickly followed by the dead man's brilliant dancing.

Each of these times, and on countless other occasions—a bad bout with flu, the birth of his son, the heart attack of a friend— he thought about death, but during those nine days he had not been *thinking* about death at all. It had not been the fear of death that had settled next to him, but the fact of it. The thing itself.

Eight years later the thing returned.

The day had been ordinary. Eddie rose with the alarm, showered, woke his son. Jennifer scrambled eggs, toasted bread. Eddie packed his and his son's lunches. While they ate, the boy told them his dream, which had to do with the trees in his schoolyard beginning to speak, reciting the alphabet and mathematical tables. The boy, Abraham Marcus for Eddie's uncle and father, had become a steady source of happiness and renewal.

Nothing in the morning drive struck Eddie as unusual. No near-accidents, no bits of shattered windshield littering the asphalt. Traffic moved responsibly. Pedestrians waited for lights to change. Eddie dropped Jennifer at the shopping mall where she managed the kitchen wares section of a department store. He took his son to elementary school. Eddie waited in the idling car until the boy disappeared with a wave into the building. Then he drove, uneventfully, to Whitman High School, where he taught American History and Civics.

The thing did not make its appearance until his third-period class.

He stood before forty students taking the roll, as was his custom, thinking about the discussion that he would presently lead—the Thirties, the Depression. Although he had taught this class a dozen times before, he could think of nothing to say now. He put away his roll book, stood before them and smiled, but the smile was insincere. It occurred to him that this course was also insincere, a superficial survey of dates and events. If the course lacked sincerity, what of his whole career as a teacher? For that matter, what in his life had meaning?

He stood in front of the class for several moments without speaking. The students grew quiet, sensing that something was wrong. He forced himself to concentrate on the material, but what was there to say, really? *The Depression was a bad time. Poverty, bankruptcies, the WPA, FDR*—all that was in the book. He felt wholly redundant and false. He could tell them that there were bread lines, but what would that mean to these kids? They would see people waiting at the door of Safeway, gabbing with their neighbors, much the way they waited in line for con-cert tickets.

The desire to break the silence finally overcame his reluctance to speak. "Comments," he said, meaning it as a question, but it came out flat and soft.

The room smelled of chalk, pencil shavings, and something darker—an earthy smell, the odor of an animal who lives by rooting in dirt. Then came another, stranger sensation—hot breath at his anus. Eddie broke out in a sweat. Death was here, this room, this moment. The breath grew warmer, followed by a gentle, urgent probing.

The young faces of his students remained calm, compliant, politely bored, like the impassive faces of snowmen. They waited, which was the nature of school, Eddie thought, waiting for something to happen. It was the very nature of life, he decided, of *his* life. He stared at the tops of his students' heads, the parts in their hair, the hip styles and odd cuts, all of which now seemed idiotic.

How would he get through this hour? The Great Depression, he reasoned, had made him depressed. This thought cheered him for a moment, then death kissed his cheek, licked the rim of his ear. Death was not a metaphor. Its coarse tongue chafed his skin.

He began to hallucinate. In the rear of the classroom, silence took a physical shape—translucent bubbles, like soap bubbles but enormous, as large as the human heads they hovered above. They multiplied like amoebas and crowded forward.

Eddie wanted to believe that he was having a breakdown. He preferred thinking this to what he knew: He was in the presence of death.

A single bubble broke free of the others and floated toward his desk, bouncing on invisible currents. Eddie saw his reflection, stretched and bloated in the sphere, the face of a drowning man. A second drifted forward. A third followed. Eddie grew short of breath.

From the back of the room came a voice. "Mr. Net?"

The bubbles vanished. In their place: a girl, one arm raised, propped up by the other, her new breasts misaligned by the raised arm's pull. "Mr. Net?" she said again.

"Yes, Cindy?" Eddie said, death, for the moment, expelled.

Rain brought out an ugly smell in the car's upholstery—cat urine. Eddie sat behind the wheel watching the yellow school buses pull away. At the corner of the gym, a boy and girl kissed. The boy, Hispanic and dark-skinned wearing a black muscle shirt, slipped one finger between the elastic waist of her skirt and the girl's hip. She broke the embrace to run for her bus, looking back at him twice. The boy stepped into the rain and waved to her as the bus departed.

Eddie turned the key in the ignition and his car came to life. He had survived his most difficult day of teaching. The switch for the windshield wipers did nothing. The fan for the vent did not work. Eddie cursed the car, an Impala, nine years old and always in need of repair.

He backed out of the parking space. The Hispanic boy yelled. Eddie had almost backed into him. "You all right?" Eddie opened his door to call to him.

"No problem," the boy said, his hair and shirt already soaked.

"Can I give you a ride somewhere?" Eddie asked him.

The boy shook his head and sauntered off through the parking lot in the rain.

Eddie drove cautiously. Drops of rain splattered against the windshield. His chest tightened, and he felt as if he might suffocate. He pulled at his collar, but it was already loose. He directed the car into a gas station and shifted into park.

Lowering the window a few inches, he pushed his head into the crack of air and inhaled heavily. Rain hit his face—warm, like the saliva of a giant beast.

What brought this on? He wondered but could find no answer. His life lacked the requisite drama for the appearance of death, and yet it had arrived. There had been his son's sixth birthday party—the typical ice cream and chaos of children. Jennifer's promotion to manager? He had felt nothing but happiness for her. The anniversary of his father's and his Uncle Abe's deaths—they had died on the same calendar day, three years apart—had recently passed, but Eddie had not thought of them, had not realized that the day grew near until it was already past.

Finally he thought of a recent trip to the doctor, an afternoon of humiliation. He'd had some shortness of breath, and an odd and painful testicular bump. His doctor—Townsend, the same man he'd seen as a child—entered and left the room several times while a nurse stayed and attended to Eddie's symptoms.

Chest X-rays came first. Then Dr. Townsend examined his ears and eyes with a penlight. He probed Eddie's mouth with a tongue depressor. Eddie lowered his pants, and Townsend bent over him to examine the bump. "Here we go," he said. "We can help you here." The bump was merely an ingrown hair. Townsend directed his nurse to remove it, while he saw other patients. "I'll be back with your chest X-rays," he told Eddie.

The nurse donned plastic see-through gloves and lifted Eddie's penis gingerly with thumb and forefinger. She squatted and stared at the bump. "You remember me?" she said.

Eddie stared between his legs at her. "I'm afraid I don't," he confessed.

"I was in your class five years ago." She stood up and let go of him. "Randi Williams, 'member?"

She reached for the metal stand at the foot of the bed. Eddie misunderstood and shook the gloved hand.

"You were my favorite teacher," she said, retrieving tweezers from the stand. "I sat in the front row next to that girl from India." She lifted his penis again. "There's pus," she announced. She began her painful pecking at the sore.

Eddie, so embarrassed that tears came to his eyes, could not look at her. "I don't recall anyone," he said, staring at the wall. "I don't remember students."

By the time Townsend returned with the X-rays, Eddie wanted only to leave. The black-and-gray negatives made him think of dark skies. "Your lungs." Townsend tapped at light ovals shrouded in black. They looked to be the size of sandwich baggies. "No fluid," Townsend said. "They're not the lungs of an athlete, but hell . . ."

"Sometimes I feel I can't catch my breath. Not often. Now and then," Eddie said.

"Just living will do that to you," Townsend explained. "You need to exercise more. Lose a few pounds. Other than that, you're no worse off than anybody else."

The episode, though degrading, could not account for what had happened today, Eddie decided. He mulled the thought over a long while, his breathing regular once more. He wiped at the fog on the windshield with his sleeve. He tried the wipers again, and they mysteriously worked.

Eddie left the window open for his drive home, arriving with drops of water clinging to his face, his shirt wet across one shoulder.

On his knees on the living-room floor, Eddie's son drew endless circles on large sheets of thick white paper. Eddie, in a dry shirt, a towel draped over one shoulder, asked him what he was drawing.

"Circles," Marc told him.

Eddie saw a face among the overlapping circles—an oblong face with drooping jowls, a clown's nose, tiny eyes where the circles overlapped. The child drew another circle. Hair appeared across the forehead, parted far to one side, and Eddie recognized the drawing. It was *his* face. The boy had drawn his father.

He kneeled and peered over Marc's shoulder. The damp towel slid down his back to the floor. Yes, he thought, it's me. A good likeness.

"Can I have it?" he asked his son. "Can I have your picture?"

Marc angled his head toward his father and smiled. He offered the pad of paper to his father. Eddie carefully tore away the top sheet. He looked at the drawing as if into a mirror. The scarred and spattered face stared back as startled and disbelieving as an ancient Spaniard.

"Jennifer," he called and hurried into the hall, where he met her just as she stepped from the bathroom. "Look what Marc drew."

She nodded. "Circles."

Eddie yanked the paper from her, and although he stared at it a long time, that was all he could now see. Circles.

On his knees beside his bed, Eddie tried to pray. "Dear God," he began, but that sounded too much like the opening of a letter. He started over. "God, what is happening to me?"

He meant to wait for a reply, but a rattling began in his chest, which made him feel foolish, and he said what people always say when they pray. "Forgive me," he whispered, then wondered what he'd do if God *did* forgive him. What then?

Jennifer stood in the doorway staring at him, her hands at her mouth. A tall and graceful woman, she had studied dance for seven years although she had no aptitude for it. All her life people had told her that she looked like a dancer, and so she had tried. Her family had been disappointed in her choice of Eddie, who was three inches shorter than she and neither athletic nor handsome. She'd called him "Steady Eddie" when they first met. His temperament, and his love, were as solid as his stocky body. It startled her to see him on his knees.

"You were praying," she said through her fingers.

Eddie stood to face her. "I think I'm dying," he told her, and as he said it, the idea earned his conviction, as if God really had answered his question. The revelation came with such power that his legs gave, and he was in danger of collapsing. He balanced himself with a hand on the mattress. Death was not only near, it would not leave until it took him with it.

"I don't believe in God anymore," Jennifer said. She dropped her hands from her mouth to her hips. "I couldn't ever find Him, and it's been so long now since I tried." She stepped around her husband and sat on the bed.

"God's not something you need to believe in," Eddie said, settling beside her. "He's either out there or He's not. What we believe won't change that a bit."

She touched his chest with one finger. "What makes you think you're sick?"

"I'm not sick, I'm dying." Saying it again increased his conviction. "There's something inside me, moving around."

This answer confused Jennifer. "Like a bug or a tapeworm?"

"Like a monkey," he said, "in a closet."

Jennifer looked down to her lap. "That's your heart," she whispered. Louder, she said, "Are you sad about our marriage?"

"No."

"Teaching? Is it teaching?"

"You're not listening."

She touched his cheek. "What is it then?"

"I'm dying and I don't want to."

He fell back against the bed. The monkey in his chest hopped against his ribs, flipped over and bounced off his stomach, somersaulted up to the base of his throat, where it pushed off again, feet first.

Eddie sat in his pajamas and slippers on the couch beside Jennifer and pretended to read a magazine. He became aware of a dark line around himself, suspended an inch above the surface of his skin. When he moved, the outline moved with him, like a huge glove. Beyond this outline was death.

Eddie tried to see through the glove. He expected the outline to blur his vision or to turn the world into a black-and-white movie. Instead, every object in the room shone brilliantly, like snow in sunlight. Even Jennifer's cigarette ashes had rich texture. Seen through the filter of death, the ashtray held black hollows and sharp peaks, white craters, stretches of gray noise.

He pressed his palms to his eyes, which had begun to ache. He felt the outline hunker closer. Beyond it, an animal waited to inhabit him. A black bear. A deer. A starfish. A red grouse.

When Eddie removed his hands from his eyes, the glove had lifted. Death had gone. The ashtray merely held ashes. For a second he detected the scent of a sweating horse, but it quickly passed.

He relaxed against the couch cushion, but now the outline surrounded his wife, dangerously close. "Don't move," he told her. Speaking made the outline vanish.

"What is it?" Jennifer asked.

Eddie needed to see their son. He leapt from the couch to find him, but his knee banged against the coffee table and the ashtray flew onto the floor, scattering Jennifer's butts and speckled ashes. He swore, and it gave him some release, so he swore again, loudly, and kicked the table over.

Marc ran into the room and to his mother. "What is Daddy doing?" he said.

Jennifer pulled him to her chest and covered his ears. "He's dying," she whispered, too softly for the boy to hear.

The psychiatrist wore a dark and dignified suit. His hair had the metallic shine of copper and was elegantly cut. He smiled politely but with restraint when Eddie introduced himself. Almost everything in the room was made of oak—oak desk, oak filing cabinet, oak chairs with leather cushions. Books on oak shelves covered one entire wall. The room smelled vaguely of moldy books.

Dr. Sayre directed him to one of the oak chairs, which relieved Eddie, as he was afraid he would have to lie on a couch.

"What do you think is wrong with you?" Dr. Sayre began.

"I think I'm dying," Eddie said plainly.

"What has led you to this conclusion?"

Eddie said, "The presence of death."

Dr. Sayre nodded and waited for him to continue, but Eddie didn't know what to add. "Let's talk about that," Sayre said. His voice carried a conversational lilt. He seemed like a friendly man.

Eddie began with the story of the nine black days following his wedding. It was a longer story than he recalled. At one point, he noticed Dr. Sayre glance to Eddie's left. While continuing the story, Eddie casually looked that way. A pendulum clock in an oak case silently counted the seconds. Eddie coughed, covering his mouth, as if this were why he had turned his head. He pretended not to know that the psychiatrist was bored. Dr. Sayre pretended not to have seen that Eddie noticed, jumping in with uncharacteristic verve when the story ended.

But when Eddie looked again at Sayre, the doctor's coppery hair had turned potato brown. His oak desk shone candy-apple red.

"It's like the world changed color," said Eddie. He thought that this sort of thing might happen all the time but you had to be dying to notice. Maybe there were advantages.

The psychologist's hair returned to normal. The oak desk became oak once more. Dr. Sayre wanted to know whether Jennifer was happy with their sex life. "Does this question make you uncomfortable?" he added.

"Yes, it makes me uncomfortable," Eddie replied.

"Describe what you're feeling."

"I don't like talking about some things. I feel when I let them out, they're less mine." As he spoke, the glove became visible.

It brushed against the fine hairs on his arm and at the base of his neck, then lightly touched the raised bones of his ribs and the seam of his scrotum. "Besides, you don't seem to care that I'm dying. But then, why should you?" Looking at Sayre now, Eddie saw a glove hovering about him, too. "I'm sorry, but you don't know me, and even if I answer all your questions, you won't know me."

"Can you explain this hostility you're expressing now?" Sayre wanted to know.

"I have to die," Eddie said.

He drove directly to school. An overweight, balding man addressed his fourth-period students. He was the worst of the substitute teachers. He never followed a lesson plan and spoke vulgarly to make the kids laugh. Normally Eddie endured him. Dying, he did not have the time.

"I'm back," he said. "You can go."

The substitute put his hands on his wide hips and glared at Eddie. The angle of his elbows turned his arms into flippers, and he became a walrus. The room began to smell of fish. Eddie laughed and said, "Get out."

As he left, a new odor entered—a dark and swampy one. Eddie felt a seam of the glove touch his spine—cool, wet. The long and narrow tongue of a reptile. A lizard? The tongue and scaly head now probed his anus for entry. A snake. A psychologist would make something of that, Eddie thought, but death was not symbolic. Death just was.

He turned to the students. Their foreheads glistened under the fluorescent lights like polished fruit. He saw the boys and girls with a clarity that would have been terrifying were he not already dying. He saw how spindly their arms were, how delicate their hands. He saw their freshly laundered, perfectly ironed blouses and purposefully tattered jeans as hopeless emblems of invincibility. He studied their faces, their somber, youthful faces.

"World War Two," he began, aware of the urgency in his voice, thinking how a mass of helmets seen from above would look like nothing more than turtle backs, how his father and Abe met by coincidence in southern Italy and held each other through the night like lovers, how they survived the war, then got old and died anyway, how his death had come to him so that he could tell these stories.

He began the telling.

Others

Leaving the TV on is something I inherited from Pop, only he left the sound up and didn't listen and I leave the picture on and don't watch. He's given up TV, but I've got it on, an old movie with men in gray suits. One has a gun. I don't know what they're doing because there's no sound, just pictures lighting up the room. I used to come home from school and find Pop doing the dishes in the kitchen with the TV blaring out front. "Keeps the boogeyman away," he'd say.

It's almost midnight. I'm still in my clothes and socks, lying on the couch with the sheet pulled up to my neck. This is the smallest place yet. It's old, too, and everything's wood—floors, walls, ceilings, stairs. Downstairs is the kitchen and family room with the TV and couch where I sleep. Everyone else sleeps upstairs. Mom worries the couch will stun my growth, but I curl up anyway, something that used to bother Pop. He told me the difference between a good man and a bad was the difference between an open hand and a fist. Curling up, I was making myself into a fist. He was real corny back then, a stage he went through for a long time. He said he was afraid I'd go bad.

I almost did. This one night I couldn't sleep, I was riding my bike up and down the alleys in the old neighborhood, looking into people's yards, peeking over fences just for something to do. I spotted a telescope on a porch, right out in the open, and in a snap I decided to take it. I climbed over the fence, but once I was in the yard I saw this sheet folded lengthwise across the clothesline. It was white and the moon was shining on it so it sort of glowed.

For some reason, the sheet stopped me. I didn't take the telescope. Once in a while, I pretend that looking at the television is like looking into a telescope—you know, like I'm really seeing something big.

The man with the gun is in a warehouse in the middle of a bunch of mannequins, being still. I don't know what he's hiding from. His eyes have that shiny look that on TV means you're scared, and his hair is getting all sweaty. Right then there's a clomp on the stairs, which scares *me* for a minute. My little sister drops one foot and then the other on the stairs, real slow, which means she's sleepy. Della is ten and wearing one of Pop's shirts, the striped tails dripping down the steps. She's wagging her head, like this is too much for her.

"It's her again," Della says and sits on the bottom stair, her bare feet peeking out from the shirt. She's little for her age, with hair the color of a paper sack and all shuffled by sleep.

"All you got to do is talk to her," I say.

Della shrugs, so I get up. I'm four years older, a foot taller, and my hands are twice as big as hers, but they aren't like a man's hands—they're soft, kind of doughy. I spend a lot of time wondering how I got these hands—like how does that get decided?

We climb the stairs together. I have to go slow because she's still half asleep. Della's going to be a dentist when she grows up so she can look inside people all she wants. She thinks everybody's secrets are waiting just past their tonsils.

Halfway up the stairs I hear the woman yelling. "I want to

speak with the father," she calls out. "Hey in there, let me speak with the father."

"You only have to talk to her a minute and she shuts up," I say.

Della doesn't even look up at me but goes right to the single bed that she shares with Rib. I can't tell whether he's asleep or just got his eyes closed. He's two and a half and has the family looks, only it's like they weren't finished. They're flattened out, like part of him still isn't born. He's got boils on his face like little plums.

Pop's awake, lying flat on the big bed, his fingers interlocked over his belly. His eyes never leave the ceiling, like something's going on up there and if he looks away he'll miss the best part. Mom's next to him, a pillow over her head. She says anymore it's the only way she can sleep.

"I want the father one to speak with me," the woman calls out.

I go right to the window. She's across the narrow alley, her window dead even with ours—a big woman in a gray night-gown, her brown hair pressed flat and greasy against her head. Her bed's next to the window, and she props herself up and yells out at us once or twice a week. Two of her bottom teeth are gone.

I yank the window up. It only takes a minute to talk with her and she'll quit. No one else likes to do it. Just the thought of it wears them out.

"What is it?" I say to her.

She looks at me all lost—like why am I bothering her?—then says, "Have you seen my Pepsi bottle?"

I say, "What?"

"Have you seen my Pepsi bottle? I can't find it anywhere. Looking, looking. Have you seen it?"

Something happens to me right then. This anger rushes up

as if it comes out of the floor. "Shut up," I yell at her. "You're waking us all up, the seven of us awake because of you. You're keeping us all up."

"I just thought you'd seen my Pepsi bottle," she says, sounding put out and hurt. The skin around her mouth flutters even when she's through talking, as if more words are gathering there.

"Don't ever call at us about any Pepsi bottle," I say and slam the window down. Della is sitting up and staring because I don't usually yell, but Rib's got his eyes shut tight, and Pop keeps on checking out the ceiling, and Mom's head is still underneath the pillow.

"Go back to sleep," I say to Della and I walk out.

Pop hasn't talked for a couple of months. Oh, he'll say yes or no, or one of our names—there's nothing wrong with his throat. He's just given it up, like he did TV. He worked construction back when. Mom worked too, before Rib was born, at the sewage-treatment plant, walking on a concrete ramp all night, checking to see that the big wheels were turning. If one of them quit, she had a button to push and a procedure to follow. She really likes that word *procedure*. She uses it for everything. Even Rib's birth she calls "a medical procedure." I don't have a word, not one I like any better than the others.

We get checks from the government now. I pump gas at Texaco after school, and when our neighbor starts bellowing, I talk with her. Usually I never yell. It's not that hard. Usually I can do it in my sleep.

I get back on the couch again. On TV, the man with the gun has moved out to the country. There are pigs and a barn. His gun must be hidden in his coat or pants or somewhere underneath things. Before I can get comfortable, Della is back on the

stairs, dancing down this time, wide awake now. At the bottom
of the stairs, she squats on the edge of the step in this funny
way she has, like a frog, and stares at me all weird.

"What is it?" I say. "She back already?"

"Who are the others?" Della says.

"What others?"

"You said she was keeping all seven of us up."

As soon as she says it, I realize she's right. I did say that.
Somehow, adding up the family, I came up with seven. Della's
looking hard at me, but I don't know what to tell her. The TV
keeps blinking pictures and the room gets quiet while I think,
but how can you explain a mistake like that?

Finally, Della says something. "I dreamed about an extra *room*
once," she says. "We all forgot it was there. It was behind the
shower." She puts her elbows on her knees, her chin in her
hands.

"Yeah?" I say, then I lock my hands behind my head and
look up at the ceiling, only there's nothing up there but wood
planks lined up one after the other, so I turn back to her.

"You ever have a dream like that?" she says.

"Sometimes I get this dream where there's these parts to us
we forgot about," I tell her. "In the dream I go, 'Oh yeah,' and
I can use this other part to do something great, like fly or turn
invisible."

Della nods and wipes hair from her face. "I had one like that.
I could look right through clothes and skin."

"What was in there?"

"Mostly bones," she says. "But they were lined up like they
spelled something—only it was a different kind of alphabet. I
couldn't read it."

"That's a weird one," I say.

On TV the man with the gun still doesn't have his gun out.
He's been wounded somehow in the chest and is hiding in the

barn. The hay around him is dark with blood. Sometimes I think how even the dark things on TV, like his coat or the blood, give off light. I could think about this a lot if Della weren't staring at me like she still wants an answer.

"I just miscounted," I say, and shrug one shoulder. "She got me mad and I counted wrong."

Della doesn't like the answer. She glares at me like I'm keeping secrets, but she gets up anyway to climb the stairs. "Goodnight, then," she says.

"Yeah," I say, and I want to say *Sorry*, but what's there to be sorry for?

I get up and turn the TV off. I figure the man with the gun's going to get out of it some way because he's the star. I don't need to watch. The television glows white before it goes dark, then I lie back, and the funny thing is—when I counted up the family, there *were* others. I look at the TV screen and try to picture them. All that shows is my reflection, partially blotted out by the dark. I close my eyes, but I still can't see them.

What I wonder is: what would they look like? They could resemble Rib, only even less there—hardly any features at all, just a few bumps and ridges. But what would they be doing here? I open my eyes and the dark kind of surprises me. I think, If it were dark enough, this room could be anywhere—it could be in the White House, it could be as big as the sky. Except it's old and has that old wood smell, along with something sort of like a grease smell from so many people rubbing up against it for so long. I pull the sheet to my chin, curl into a fist. Then I wonder, What would the others do nights *they* couldn't sleep? The couch springs make a sound when I move, like someone breathing. And on nights they could sleep, where would they find to lie down?

Salt Commons

As it pulled to a stop the car crested the curb, its rusted bumper brushing against Paul Hosea's pantleg. Paul anticipated a friend and the offer of a ride, as it was a cold spring morning. He bent to look through the car window. A heavyset woman sat behind the wheel. She wore a plaid hunting jacket. When Paul's face came level with hers, she showed him the gun. A shiny revolver. "Get in," she said.

His knees faltered, tossing him backward. He grabbed the rear door handle to keep from falling. The eye of the gun studied him unsympathetically.

He climbed into the backseat, but the woman said, "Up here." Paul threw his leg over, straddling the back of the seat, then rolled clumsily into the front beside her. He was a tall and frail man entering middle age much as he had the car—gracelessly and alone.

While he settled himself in the seat, the woman stared fixedly at his face, as if deciding something. Paul had not aged especially well—he had trouble with his skin and teeth. On Sunday mornings, he bent over his bathroom sink and dyed his hair black. The unnatural darkness contrasted with his pale features to give him a funereal appearance.

"You're going to help me," the woman told him, and the car

began to move. She steered with her right hand, which was gloved, maneuvering the wheel with an air of indifference that terrified Paul, as if kidnaping a man at gunpoint were no more unusual than taking a bath or frying a chicken. Her left hand was not gloved, resting in her lap, aiming the pistol at his chest. Each finger flaunted a simple gold ring.

She executed a U-turn and began heading toward Adams River. The stillness of the morning sky became portentous. A single cardinal flying from the naked limbs of a giant oak to a maple's bare branches seemed, to Paul, to tell the story of his life. He saw a dog sniffing at a sewer drain, and suddenly this, too, embodied his history.

"I'm trying to find one of your neighbors." The woman's gruff voice shaded her words with threat. "I've got the address wrong. There's no such place as what I was looking for."

"Did you try the phone book?" Paul asked her. His voice sounded thin and tremulous, even to him.

"Unlisted. You think I'm stupid?"

"I wish I could help you." He tried to sound friendly. "But I really should get to work."

The woman's expression underwent a dramatic change. She had thick eyebrows, which she now raised in amusement. "You won't be able to make it today," she told him cheerfully. "You have some sick pay coming? Let's hope you do."

He didn't think he could overwhelm her. He was not very good at physical things. Besides, she weighed more than he did and looked to be stronger. "My name is Paul Hosea," he said. "I work at Skinner's Grocery. I'm not married." If she got to know him, she would have more trouble killing him—if killing him was what she planned to do. "I have two brothers," he went on. "One's a schoolteacher in Stapleton. The other's a mechanic in Kearney."

"Pleasure's all mine, I'm sure." She steered the car onto the gravel road by the river without slowing down. The rear end fishtailed, then righted itself. A ribbon of dust trailed them. Rocks ticked against the muffler. The road quickly took them out of Salt Commons. They seemed to be the only thing in the landscape that moved.

At the river's bend, she slowed and pulled onto the shoulder overlooking the water. Paul could see no human form distant or near. Gaps in the trees that bordered the far banks of the river revealed plowed fields and grazing land, a few white-face cows staring blankly in their direction. The river splayed around an isle of mud at the bend. Weeds grew along the edge, gray from the spring chill. The tallest brushed against the car's belly.

"I want you to look at this." She removed her wallet from the rear pocket of her jeans. She had to raise herself in the car seat to do this, and the pistol tumbled to the floorboard by her feet.

She made no move for the gun, but looked Paul steadily in the eyes.

He returned her stare, as if the loose pistol did not exist. "I don't like guns," he said. "I want to cooperate with you. We don't need that thing."

She squinted in approval, showing her teeth. "I like a cautious man," she said. "They last longer." She retrieved the revolver.

From her wallet she withdrew a wrinkled photograph of a man and woman holding hands. Paul recognized the two. The man was Miller Klokker, a pharmacist nearing fifty, married with four children, the oldest of whom worked at the video store next door to Skinner's. The Klokkers lived down the street from Paul. The woman, Lu Tao, was the wife of the county superintendent of schools. In her middle thirties, Paul guessed, although she looked younger in the photograph. Her only child, a four-year-old, had Down's syndrome.

"Are these people from around here?" Paul meant to sound

offhand, but it came out more theatrical than he intended. "I know most of the people who live around here. Nebraska is sprinkled with little towns. Are you sure Salt Commons is the right place?"

She smiled again, tapping the ignition key against her teeth. "I'm sure." She pursed her lips and shook her head, staring past him at the shallow water. "Not much of a river, is it?"

"A cousin of mine drowned in the Adams," Paul offered. "Years ago. Dove into an eddy that turned out to be only a foot or so deep. Broke her neck and drowned."

"Pity." She took the photograph from him and waved it in the space between them. "You don't know these people, mister, I'm going to have to kill you."

"Please," he said, his voice cracking. "Please, call me Paul."

"Paul, you don't lie well. It doesn't suit you." She laughed— a harsh sound, like a crow coughing. "I bet there's not a dozen people in Salt Commons you don't know. You want to bet? What have you got that we could bet?"

"I have a car," he said. "A Pontiac. Nicer than this one."

"You don't like my car?" She pretended to be hurt, and he saw that she was a young woman, which gave him a flicker of hope.

"Miller Klokker," she said, pointing at the photo. "Lu Tao. That light any rooms up there?" She pointed with the barrel of the pistol at his head.

"No," he insisted. Even though the car was cold, a stream of dark sweat trickled down his temple. "I wish I got out more, knew more people."

Again she tapped her teeth with the key. Her teeth were short and had deep ridges. "You live by yourself?"

"I never married," Paul said. "I fell in love with a woman who lives in Kearney, but she chose another man." He paused, not wanting her to think that no one would care if he died. "I still have hopes of finding someone. I keep myself in good condition. I exercise and walk to work." He had read that soldiers never referred to their enemies as people. They transformed them into gooks, savages. Snuffing out life was not easy. "I've loved one woman most of my life."

"Let's visit your house, Paul," she said. "Do you feel like entertaining?"

"You need to turn around," he told her, and she began steering the car. "I live just a block from the river. I like to be near the water." A lump had formed in his throat, and it was painful to swallow.

On the way back to town, she slowed almost to a stop and pointed with the pistol out the passenger window. "What's that out there?"

"It's a salt flat," Paul explained. "It's the reason for our name."

Barren and vaguely yellow, the salt flat spread from the muddy lip of Adams River like a terrestrial canker. Immense hickories and elms surrounded it. Beyond them, the dark earth rippled uniformly—corn fields come spring. The sudden trees encircling it, their gray limbs lifted reverently, set it off from the farmland. They lent to it the air of a shrine.

"It looks like a place to play ball—an infield," she said. The few scraps of coarse grass scattered over the surface lifted and fell as a cold wind passed. The morning sun made the ground glitter.

Paul asked, "What should I call you?"

She pressed the accelerator and thought for several moments while they sped down the gravel road. "Let's say my name is Jane." Her heavy brows rose again. "You want me to call you Tarzan?"

He didn't think to laugh. "Some of my friends call me Hosea, but most people use Paul." Then he added, "Hosea is a biblical name."

"So is Jane," she said. "There must be a Jane in there some-where."

"You don't lock your door, Paul?" Jane prodded his back with the pistol as they stepped together over the threshold. "That's the kind of town this is?"

With the blinds shut, the small front room seemed gloomy. Paul switched on the overhead light. "There's no crime in Salt Commons," he said. "Nothing to speak of."

"Are you trying to make me feel bad?" she asked him. "Where are your manners?" She squinted once more, then said, "Where's your phone?"

In the little drawer of the phone stand, she found Paul's address book. She removed her black leather gloves to look up Miller Klokker. The gold rings on both hands clicked softly as she fingered the pages, like tumblers in a lock.

She said, "This Klokker even lives on your street, doesn't he? One-thirty-nine Iroquois Drive. That can't be more than three blocks."

Paul felt a new wave of panic grip his throat and now his stomach, too. "Yes," he said, "Iroquois Drive. I don't know why it's called that. Salt Commons was an Indian village before white people came, but not Iroquois, of course. Kiowa, I think. I liked history in school—high school, I mean. I never had the chance to go to college."

Jane's head was cocked to one side, and she examined him with one eye shut. "That's a pity," she said.

She telephoned the drugstore and found that it closed at five. She guessed that Klokker would be home by six. "The woman doesn't matter," she told Paul. "She just happened to be in the photograph." They sat so near each other their knees almost touched: Paul on the leather sofa, Jane in the matching chair.

"What's going to happen to Miller?" Paul asked.

"Same thing that happens to all of us sooner or later."

"I see." He crouched forward with his legs crossed and tried to concentrate on his predicament, but a dirty shirt left on the back of the rocker troubled him. He felt a strong urge to tidy up.

Jane said, "What do you figure Klokker would be thinking if he knew this was his last day with the living?"

Paul shook his head without speaking. He knew that this was likely *his* last day among the living. It seemed that his thoughts should be grander; all he could focus on was the dirty shirt on the rocker and possible ways he might survive.

"I know what I'd be thinking," Jane said. "I'd be making a list of all the men I ever slept with and all the people I ever killed. Those are the most profound connections you can make with a person."

She seemed to be bragging, but maybe she was hinting. "Would you like to sleep with me?" Paul asked her.

"No, sir. Thank you, anyway."

"Are you going to kill me?"

"Likely as not."

He looked up at the ceiling, his hand at his slender throat, the little knobs of his Adam's apple. "Then it's true? I will never again make love with a woman?"

"Your time for that has passed," she said.

"I won't ever cook another meal? I won't swim again. I'll never see the ocean."

"It's funny, isn't it? Something you can't even imagine becomes real just like that." She snapped her fingers.

"Why are you going to kill Miller Klokker?"

"He's a bad man."

"Why are you going to kill me?"

"Because you stopped on the way to work to help out a stranger. For that, you're going to die. Hardly fair, is it? The way things are, there's no real living anymore, just survival. Stopping for me, that was a survival error."

The injustice of this angered him. He stood to demand his release, but Jane fired her pistol into the couch. The sound was sharp though not loud. Paul sat immediately.

"You're going to stay right there," Jane told him.

The hole in the white leather was oblong. The bullet had entered at an angle.

While he sat in his living room that long morning, Paul thought of the women he had slept with. The measly list did not include the sole woman he had ever loved. Only once did he have a real opportunity. It had not been during their failed courtship, decades ago, when they both had been young and full of desire, but last August, the month he'd begun dyeing his hair.

She surprised him by appearing at the grocery. She lived thirty miles away, and he hadn't seen her in more than a year. Overdressed and heavily made-up, she waited until there were no customers, then asked him to meet her that evening.

They drove around town in his car. While the Pontiac's headlights revealed the familiar streets, she confessed that she had left her husband.

The night had been warm and humid, with a light breeze off the river. Paul followed the dirt road that led to the old Watlings home, gutted years ago by fire, and now little more than a charred foundation. In the dark, on the wide front seat of his sedan, he lay across his true love, stroking her hair, kissing her lips. But the wind changed direction and brought the stench of the stockyard, which made it impossible for him to continue.

"Come home with me," he said. She nodded and kissed the lids of his eyes; later that night, alone in his house, Paul would see the smears of lipstick left by her gentle mouth.

He steered the Pontiac to his clapboard house. In his front yard sat her husband, his legs extended before him on the lush grass—the posture of a chastened child. He rose and shook Paul's hand, as if Paul were merely delivering her. "I'm ashamed of myself," he said. He took his wife's hand and kissed it tenderly. "Nothing's happened that can't be forgotten," he said to her. "What we can't forgive, we can just forget."

Tears appeared on her cheeks, and Paul lost her once again.

"I've got to eat something." Jane motioned with the pistol for Paul to stand. "Let's see what's in your kitchen."

They settled on soup—beef and vegetable—out of a can. Paul put it on a burner, then asked permission to go to the bathroom.

"As long as you don't mind company," she said.

"I do mind."

"Then you better hold it. Myself, I can go all day. Big woman, big bladder. Comes in handy when you do a lot of traveling."

While they ate, Jane talked about Arizona. "Right now in Phoenix it's probably eighty-three degrees. I lived there for sixteen months." She told him about cactus and men in short pants and mountains where there were gold mines that no one could find. "Why do you live in a place like this when you could live in a place like that?" she asked him.

"I don't know," he answered honestly. "I was born near here. I've meant to travel." Then he added, "I still hope to."

"I've been in thirty-nine states," Jane said, "plus D.C., Mexico, Canada. I've seen the Grand Canyon, Niagara, Yosemite, Statue of Liberty, Mount Rushmore, White Sands, Lincoln Memorial. Truth is, it all looked better on TV. All of it. There's no real living the way there used to be. Every now and then you get a moment of pleasure. Take it where you find it. The rest is pure survival. Sometimes I think God is going to raise up his old head and yell, 'Get on with it! What do you think I made this all up for?' " She sighed, resigned. "Of course, that won't happen."

"Do you have children?" Paul asked her.

"Barren as the moon," she said, "and happy for it."

"And those rings?"

Jane wiggled her fingers on one hand, passed the gun to the other, and wiggled the remaining fingers. "A person like me doesn't have much to spend her money on. 'Plain gold,' I told the jeweler. No curlicues. Let gold be gold, I say."

An hour after their meal, Paul stood before his toilet to pee, the gun prodding his spine. "All bathrooms have windows," Jane told him. "Not about to let you run off." She laughed when she heard his splash. "We're getting to be like old buddies."

Paul imagined that the time remaining for condemned men passed quickly, that anything so valuable must slip away. But the afternoon dragged on and on. He found himself wishing for something to happen—anything, good or bad.

"Is there any chance you'll let me go?" he asked her. "If I cooperate?"

They hadn't spoken for several minutes. Jane looked at him as if she had forgotten he was in the room. "Depends on my whims," she said. "It's possible. Is that a rug?" She was eying at his hair.

"It's mine," he said. Embarrassed, he tugged at a handful. "I dye it," he admitted, then cleared his throat, further embarrassed. He had told no one this, although, he realized now, the truth was obvious enough.

"It makes you look foolish," she said.

"I've tried to live my life correctly," he told her, suddenly angry. "I've tried to have values."

"What's that have to do with coloring your hair?"

"All right, I have some vanity. Who doesn't? But I've tried to live according to the rules of society."

"You're ancient history," Jane said. "You're already extinct."

"Let me wash it," Paul said. "I'd rather not die with this in my hair."

"It'll leach right into the soil. They'll find you all gray and think, He must've been scared to death!" She laughed her raucous laugh. "Might as well keep your sense of humor, Paul."

He said, "I don't see the point in your killing me."

"Well," Jane said, "I don't see the point in your living."

At six, they drove to the house of Miller Klokker. Paul considered flinging open the door and falling to the asphalt, but it seemed unreal and impossible, and he would likely be shot; while, if he behaved, she might just tie him up or take him along and drop him off in the middle of nowhere. If she knew him, she couldn't kill him, he told himself again, but it no longer carried the ring of truth.

They stood before the Klokkers' house like a married couple. Paul prayed that it would not be a child who came to the door. This prayer was answered. Miller smiled at him, then looked at Jane, who displayed the gun.

"You been expecting me?" she said.

Miller held a dish towel in his hands, which he ran over his large knuckles and long fingers, then dropped onto the beige carpet. He joined them outside, closing the door behind him. He was a big man with powerful shoulders, but his hair was gray and the skin beneath his chin was flaccid like the dewlap of a cow.

"The wife is in the kitchen," he whispered. "She hasn't seen you. No need to involve her."

"Let's go for a spin," Jane said.

They walked Indian file to the car. Jane produced a pair of handcuffs from the glovebox. She linked them through an armrest and then around Miller's wrists. Paul sat in the middle.

Again they headed toward the river.

"Well, Paul," Miller said, but he didn't follow it up.

"The famous innocent bystander," Jane explained. "Truth is, he's not as innocent as you might think." She gave Paul a sidelong glance. "Tried to trade his body for a break."

Miller shook his head. "We all do what we must to get by." To Paul he added, "I'm sorry."

The river was as still as ice, but the water was not frozen and reflected the darkening sky. Jane veered off the road and onto the salt flat. Her car lugged, the engine straining over the soft ground. She parked near the trees at the far end, leaving the parking lights on. Paul trailed her out of the car, as she instructed, and removed a shovel from the cluttered trunk.

"I like this place," she said. "It isn't the Grand Canyon, but it's as close to a tourist spot as you've got around here." She looked steadily at Paul, waiting until he met her eyes. She said, "Pick your spot of eternal rest."

"I don't want to die," he said.

"Not a one of us do," she said.

He nodded. "Then I'd prefer to be by the river."

"Nah," she said, "too close to the road. They'll find your body after a while and put you in the cemetery anyway." She opened the passenger door, causing Miller to tumble onto the salty earth. "We'll make him dig," she told Paul, snickering as if they were friends. To Klokker she said, "First you dig your friend's grave, then you'll cover him up and dig your own." She put the pistol in Miller's ear while she unlocked the handcuffs.

They settled on a site. Jane handed Miller the spade. "Start digging," she said. "Do a good job. You don't want to enter the ever-after as a goldbrick."

Miller nodded somberly, then whirled and slapped her head with the blade of the shovel. The gun fell from her hand without firing. She crumpled. Miller dove for the pistol, but Jane was unconscious and could make no move for it.

Paul dropped to his knees. He was not going to die. Tears filled his eyes. "I thought we were dead." He put his hand to his heart. "I really thought we were done for."

"A hell of a close call," Miller agreed. He sighed, crouching over Jane, the pistol already in his belt. The soft skin beneath his neck rocked slightly as he removed the car keys from her coat. He glanced up at Paul. His eyes, Paul could see, were blue. "I've got to kill her, you know." He shrugged and made a frown. "There's a lot of trouble around and some of it has rubbed off on me. I can't explain. You wouldn't want to know."

Paul felt suddenly dizzy. He retrieved the shovel and held it blade up, like a scepter. The sun was completely down now, and already the moon shone brightly above him. "I'd rather you didn't kill her."

Miller took hold of the shovel just below Paul's hand. "I've got to," he said.

"She used to live in Arizona," Paul said. "She's seen the Grand Canyon."

"I've seen it myself." Miller yanked the shovel free. "Hell of a sight." He raised the blade high, and brought it down fiercely on Jane's skull. Paul turned away just before the impact. The sound was that of an axe chopping into green wood.

Instinctively, Paul scanned the area for witnesses, looking first at the dilapidated car, the steady glow of its parking lights, and then into the darkness beyond the clearing, where the river lay. No one could see them.

Jane's pistol rode in Miller's belt as if it were a perfectly natural thing for a man to carry. The soil around her wide hips grew dark with urine. Big woman, big bladder. Paul felt he might weep.

Miller bent over the body again, removing the rings from her fingers while the car's cooling engine made little clicks.

The terror that only recently had abandoned Paul spiraled anew up his spine. It made him tired. Nauseated. "I keep myself in good condition," he said softly. "I exercise, walk to work every morning."

Miller looked him up and down. "You'll get your turn to dig." He planted the blade into the earth and overturned the first shovel of salty dirt. He worked steadily, pausing only to check the gun's clip and verify that it was loaded.

He has been my neighbor for fifteen years, Paul thought. He couldn't possibly kill me. "You know, I loved a woman," Paul said, hearing a strangeness in the words as he spoke them, "but she married someone else."

"And now here you are at the salt lick with a dead body at your feet," Miller said, as if one thing naturally followed the other.

The crust of the earth was soft, but just beneath the surface it hardened. Paul hugged himself against the cold but did not want to sit in the car. He watched his neighbor dig the grave. How could he think that they knew each other? He was going to die, after all. He was as good as dead.

"Let me take a turn," Paul said. Show you're part of the effort, he thought.

Miller agreed, stepping up from the hole and tossing the shovel at Paul's feet. "Tough ground," he said. "Slow going."

Paul plunged the shovel down with both hands. He dug into the salty earth as if it were his calling, as if it were the first real work he'd ever known.

Beneath the heavy chrome bumper, the car's amber lights glowed dimly but steadily. Miller smoked a cigarette and flicked the ashes into the growing hole. Embers glowed momentarily at Paul's feet. He worked the spade, his stomach knotted with a specific terror—that he was digging his own grave. It surprised him that the feeling was not altogether foreign.

The overturned ground smelled sharp: salt, sweat, urine. His muscles ached with use. "There's something about this I like," he said suddenly, perspiration leaving long, black trails across his forehead and down his cheeks.

Miller nodded, his face lit by the cigarette's glow. "Digging makes you an accessory after the fact."

Paul stopped working and stared at Miller, but he thought of the woman he loved—what gall she'd had coming to him, as if he had nothing to do with his life but wait for her. The next thought sent a shiver through him: he wished he were burying her.

"You tired?" Miller asked.

Paul ran his arm across his face. The sleeve came away smeared with dye. "I may move to Arizona," he said.

"Not necessary." Miller flicked his cigarette butt into the hole. It landed on Paul's shoe.

Paul used the shovel to brace himself as he climbed out, then he offered it to Miller. "Just drop it there in the hole," Miller said. He waited until Paul stepped away to pick up the shovel and begin digging again.

The night had become wintry. Paul knelt beside the body and unbuttoned Jane's hunting jacket. He tugged one sleeve free, but the tail of the coat was soaked with urine, and he let it go. Jane's eyes were open; they seemed focused on him. Gently, he pressed against her lids and pushed them shut. The tips of his fingers brushed across her face and touched her lips. He slipped a finger inside her mouth and ran it across the ridges of her teeth.

The body was big. They would trade off with the shovel several times. Their shoes and socks, the cuffs of their pants would become dusted with salt. The grave would grow large enough for two. The night would grow colder and more hushed, until there was only the sound of the digging—man's work—and the creaking of the trees as the weather turned bitter.

Grief

Only Fran Schaefer's oldest clothes fit her, as if she had lost not only weight but age. She wore a dress that Lyle had given her the Christmas she was hugely pregnant with their second daughter. "I know you can't wear it now," he had said. "It's for later." Eighteen years later, it fit her perfectly.

She found Lyle in the kitchen by the sink. While she watched, he withdrew a mounded teaspoon from a box of baking soda and thrust it into his mouth. He recoiled immediately, flinging the spoon into the sink.

"You're acting crazy," Fran said. "If you have to see a doctor, you should go. Don't stay on my account."

Lyle rinsed his mouth at the sink and spat. "You can't believe the pain," he said. His hand pressed against his pale shirt, his burning stomach. "But I can manage it. I'm certain it will let up." He had been to the emergency room three times since their daughter's accident. It had been he who drove to Tucson and identified the body, who made the funeral arrangements, who told their friends. Fran believed this pain in his stomach was the price he paid.

"You should have gone to the hospital an hour ago," she said.

Grief

"I arranged the crackers on the tray," he said. "I sliced the gouda. I want to be here with you."

Although pain coarsened his voice, it sounded tranquil. His steady composure frustrated her. "You should go," she said. "You're no good to me like this. Shall I drive you?"

"No," he said, giving in. "You need to see him. Once you see him, you'll get over this . . . this way you feel about Scott." He moaned and massaged his midsection. "I hate to be at the mercy of my body."

"Make them give you something for the pain."

In the six months since the death of their first-born daughter they had been models of sanity, their feelings turbulent but their actions utterly rational. Tonight, at Lyle's insistence, they were even having the boy over, the boy who had killed her. Compulsively, Fran imagined the moment when Scott's attention wavered and the car slid off the mountain road. In one version his hand burnishes Sarah's bare thigh. In the next, they are studying for mid-terms, his eyes wandering from the road to the text she holds in her lap. All end the same way: he loses control of the car and Fran's daughter disappears.

On the day of the funeral, at the grave site, Scott had walked across the sloping wet grass to their car. He had raised his arms and stretched sheets of newspaper like flimsy wings over his head to protect himself from the drizzle.

Lyle had been leaning against the steering wheel and did not see Scott approaching, but Fran reached across the seat and lowered the window an inch. "Please leave us alone," she said.

Vi, their teenage daughter, clutched Fran's shoulder from the backseat. "Can't you see he's suffering?" Streaked by tears, her makeup had turned her face into a parody of grief.

Now, when Fran answered the door, Vi stood on the concrete walk alone. For a hopeful moment, Fran thought that Scott had backed out. "He's waiting in the car," Vi said, her eyes darting toward the dark Celica at the edge of the yard. "I wanted to make sure you were . . ." She glanced around the room.

"Your father's gone to the hospital," Fran said. "His stomach."

"Poor Daddy." Vi blinked miserably. "Can you do this without him?" In one hand she held a flat pastry, half-eaten. Fran took her wrist, as if to inspect it. "We were eating Pop-Tarts," Vi said. "It's the last thing I need, I know." She had gained ten pounds since she began seeing Scott. Fran thought that she must be taking birth-control pills.

"Tell him to come in." Fran dropped her daughter's wrist. "Leave your Pop-Tarts in the car. I've made a platter of cheeses for you." She gave her daughter a little push to get her moving.

Scott had gained weight, too. His face had grown pudgy, and his hips had the roundness of a girl's. His presence made Fran think of Sarah, of Sarah and Scott framed by this same door—tramping in from school, making an entrance in their prom clothes, coming home from their first year of college.

"Hi, Mrs. Schaefer," Scott said seriously. He handed Fran a bouquet of yellow roses wrapped in tissue paper. Vi watched from the door, leaning against the jamb, her knee raised—a pose from a lingerie ad.

The car had tumbled twenty-eight feet down the mountainside. Sarah's neck was broken, although it was not clear that she had died instantly. Scott suffered scratches, bruises, a chipped tooth, one long cut down the center of his back which required stitches. Now, he smiled uneasily, the chipped tooth turning his mouth into a vulgar thing, a lapse in decorum.

Vi joined him. They looked unhappy, Fran thought, and slightly deranged, like those hopeless and ashamed couples held together by violence. Fran said, "I should put these in water." She nosed the flowers without inhaling and hurried into the kitchen.

Grief

* * *

"I'd been in the doghouse." Scott ate the last of the cheese as he recounted his "greatest moment in sports." "I finally got to play when one of our guys, Mick Hernandez—"

Vi interrupted, "Oh, I remember him." They sat so close together their shoulders rubbed.

"Mick was low-bridged. That means the guy cut under him during a lay-up, and Mick landed on his back. It's dirty play. The unwritten rule is, whoever replaces the hurt player has to take out the other guy."

"How terrible!" Vi said.

From the tone of her daughter's voice, Fran determined that she had heard the story before.

"I've got to do something to him, but I don't want to get thrown out of the game. Did I mention I was in the doghouse?"

"Yes, you said that before," Fran said flatly. It came out uglier than she had intended.

"I pretended to go for the ball and flew into the guy, knocking him down. The acting worked. I was called for a foul, but the ref didn't toss me out. I was so pleased until I saw Mick Hernandez coming out to shake my hand. When the ref saw that, he kicked me out of the game. And that was my greatest moment in sports."

Vi laughed too loudly, rocking back and forth on the couch. She kissed him on the cheek, leaving a trace of saliva.

The story offended Fran, its false modesty and glib self-congratulation. "You boys," she began, "you have such peculiar rites."

"What do you mean?" Vi asked.

"All the secret rules they have," Fran said. "These obligations and substitutions, this eye-for-an-eye business."

"Yeah, that's true." Scott nodded, the ragged tooth betraying his smile. "It's hard to, you know, understand what you're supposed to do."

"I can see that," Fran said. "I can see that's hard for you to understand."

"Mom," Vi said. Her eyes suddenly glossed with tears.

"It's okay," Scott said. "I haven't had the chance to say, to tell you—"

Fran rose suddenly from the chair. "I have to rest now. I hope you enjoyed the cheese." With her back to them, she added, "Thank you for the flowers."

Lyle returned minutes after they left. He had not seen a doctor but fallen asleep on a couch in the waiting room. By the time he awoke, the pain had subsided.

"Scott annoyed me," Fran said. "I don't think he would have come in if you'd been here."

"Think about what you're saying." His voice was calm, patient. They sat on the couch where Vi and Scott had sat earlier. "I was the one couldn't make it."

"He sent Vi to the door to check."

Lyle let his head rest against the back of the couch. "Anyone could have been driving that car," he said. "*I* could have been. Would you hate me if I had been driving?"

Fran did not know how to answer. She felt privy to a hidden logic that permitted her to see Scott as he really was. "So you think it's healthy for Vi to be dating Sarah's old boyfriend?"

"No, of course not." He shifted uneasily on the couch. "But you and I both know better than to tell a high-school senior— or anyone, for that matter—who she should and shouldn't love." He brushed her face with the tips of his fingers. "As I recall, your parents tried to warn you about me."

Grief

Fran would not be mollified. "I don't hate him," she said. "My feelings are more specific than that." She wanted to repeat Scott's story. *Low-bridged*—it even sounded vehicular.

"I remember this dress," he said, touching the fabric just above her knee. "He brought you roses," he added. They stood in a vase on the bookshelf.

"Yes," Fran said, "he got that much right."

SPRING

On the day of Vi's graduation, Fran sold a three-bedroom house, a lot near the new mall, and a parcel of farmland next to the city dump. If all the sales closed, it would be her most productive day since she began selling real estate.

She met Lyle at the gate to the football field. An amplified voice already echoed from the temporary stage, and Fran apologized for being late.

Lyle took her arm. "Just got here myself." He led her to the bleachers. Below them, a sea of red gowns and square caps undulated in the mild wind. Fran searched for Vi, going over each row twice before spotting her. She looked haggard, fat. *That boy is killing her*, Fran thought. She shifted her gaze to the crowd of onlookers. "Let's move up higher," she said.

From the top bleacher, she was able to locate Scott's squarish head. A dark ellipse of sweat marked the space between his shoulder blades and trailed down his back. She had not seen him since he'd brought her flowers.

"That was remarkably tedious," Lyle said.

The droning had stopped. The school principal stepped down, and a student was introduced. "Scott's here," she said.

"That's hardly a surprise," Lyle said.

A waifish girl with a warbling voice began talking about "responsibility in the larger sense of the word and in the larger world." Her pale throat seemed to have the same circumference as her head.

"Did you sell the town dump?" Lyle asked.

"I wasn't offering the dump but the plot next to it," Fran said. "Yes, I sold it."

"You're on a roll."

She'd had more sales in the past several months than in the sum of the two years before. It did not escape her that this coincided with her daughter's death; rather, it made perfect sense. She worked obsessively to avoid thinking of Sarah. She and Lyle had sat here just two years before to watch Sarah graduate—to watch Sarah and Scott. It had been impossible to say her name without saying his.

"I'm very proud of her," Lyle said.

It took Fran a moment to determine about whom he was speaking, but, of course, it was Vi's graduation, and he was staring at their daughter.

The big-throated girl continued talking about the world, about disappearing species, about the carrier pigeon. Fran had to strain to make sense of it, but she was touched by the earnestness. She placed her hand on Lyle's shoulder. "Do you believe in luck?"

"Luck?" Lyle said. "I didn't know that was something one had to believe in."

"I keep thinking this has to do with luck. Not ours, *his*."

"Are you talking about Scott? We're not here to talk about Scott." Then he added, "What good does thinking like that do you?"

Fran felt the response in her body, a powerful, irrefutable argument that lived within her. *The boy's luck has run out.*

On stage, the girl began quoting Darwin—teary-eyed, her voice about to break, as if natural selection were an ongoing tragedy.

Grief

* * *

The morning after graduation, Vi announced that she was moving across the state to Tucson. She would attend summer school at the same university her sister had attended. Scott, who had dropped out following Sarah's death, had enrolled again.

"What brought this on?" Fran asked.

"We're going to live together," she said. "We're working our way back—"

"Back to what?" Fran demanded.

"Back to happiness," Vi said. "I loved Sarah and so did Scott. That ties us together like you can't imagine. It's like that song—"

"It's not like any song," Fran said. "I don't want to hear about a song."

The evening Vi moved out, Lyle took Fran to dinner. He didn't want her in the house when Scott arrived. "I don't like to see you torture yourself," he explained. "She's a big girl. We have to trust her."

"Sarah was a big girl, too," Fran reminded him.

"We all miss Sarah," he said.

The sadness in his voice kept her from saying more, but she wondered whether Scott really did miss her. One sister had replaced the other so quickly.

The salad dressing was nothing but vinegar, the soup strangely sour, the prime rib overcooked. Fran railed at the waiter. "You should be ashamed," she said. "This is an atrocity."

He offered to bring her another meal, but Lyle cut him off. "How about another round of drinks, instead? We know this isn't your fault." The waiter thanked him and left. Lyle immediately took Fran's hand. "This used to be a good place. First-rate."

"I remember." She pulled her hand away. His meddling affronted her. Lyle was a good husband, a good person, but the food had been miserable and, besides, she didn't wish to be there. Lyle could not understand that she *wanted* to watch Scott traipse through their house. She *wanted* to see Scott carrying Vi's yellow comforter, her suitcases of jeans and skirts and sweaters. A kind of torture, Lyle had called it, but, Fran thought, an essential one.

Late in the meal, Lyle suddenly admitted, "I'd like to hate Scott, but I can't. I can't find it in me to hate him." He slouched in the padded booth, his face slack from liquor, marked with dark patches. "I'd like to, though."

They had to call a cab to take them home.

AUTUMN

Before Scott's parents made the drive to Tucson, they stopped by on Thanksgiving morning to pick up some of Vi's things.

Fran had not spoken with the Edels since the night of the accident. Caroline Edel had been the one who called. Weeping, hoarse with tears, she had said, "Scottie and Sarah have had a wreck." Then, "We've lost Sarah."

Caroline pecked Lyle's cheek at the door, then turned to Fran and took her into her arms. "You look wonderful," she said to Fran. "There's not a line on your face." Caroline did not look well herself: a pocket of flesh below one eye deformed the shape of it, making it droop, and a grayness loomed beneath her thin hair—probably a bad dye job, but it gave the impression of something worse, as if her skull had discolored.

Her husband waited in the car. "His back is troubling him no end," she said, and Lyle dutifully began carrying Vi's bags to the station wagon. Meanwhile, Caroline kept up a constant prattle, which Fran found herself enjoying. She watched Lyle through the window, leaning against the station wagon, talking.

It seemed like forever since they'd had a simple conversation with friends.

The Edels didn't stay long. As Caroline was about to leave, Fran gave her a hug. While she was close, Caroline whispered, "We've loved both your daughters." It was not a mean thing to say, but it struck Fran as wrong somehow. She wanted to talk to Lyle about it, but he was drinking a gin fizz and watching football.

"I'm going shopping," she told him.

"It's Thanksgiving," he said.

"Everything is open all the time now," she said. "Don't you keep track of the world?"

He didn't respond, but switched the channels from one football game to another.

Almost every store was closed. Eventually she found a department store across from the hospital. Among the few people milling about was Ginger Waithe—the girl Scott had been dating when he fell for Sarah. It occurred to Fran that if Ginger had found a way to keep Scott, Sarah would be alive. Thinking this disturbed her, and she wondered, instead, whether there had been some common element in Ginger, Sarah, and Vi that made them attractive to Scott, or was it always merely circumstance, coincidence, convenience?

Ginger caught sight of her and headed down the aisle. "I'm so sorry about Sarah."

Fran nodded patiently. "I know."

"I wish . . ." Her sentence ended in the shaking of her head, the shifting of her honey hair. "I was at school. I couldn't come to the funeral. I live in Berkeley now."

"Home visiting your parents?"

"My mother had a stroke." Ginger's eyes fluttered suddenly, as if she were flirting with a boy or blinking back tears. "But it's okay. She's going to be all right."

They talked briefly about the hospital, therapy, temporary paralysis, the stages of Denial, Anger, Rage. In another moment, the conversation seemed over, but Ginger raised her chin, angled it toward Fran. "I hear that Viola . . . that she and Scott . . ."

"They're living together," Fran said.

Ginger's chin dropped to her chest, the honey hair cutting a slash across her jaw. She still cared for Scott. Sarah dead, her own mother hospitalized, but what affected the girl was that Scott loved someone else.

"What is it about him?" Fran demanded. "What is it about Scott Edel that makes him so special?"

Ginger was shocked. "Don't you know?" she asked. "Isn't it obvious? Why Mrs. Schaefer . . ." Her eyes enlarged, the beginnings of a smile contorted her lips. "It's almost like . . ." She looked up suddenly, as if she expected to see Scott among the dirty ceiling tiles. "It's almost like he's too good to be true."

The ceiling tiles were matted, white, and feathery, but with a dirty hue—grimy from the fumes of people's lives.

WINTER

Lyle asked Fran to accompany him to Philadelphia for Christmas. His mother was ailing; she was eighty-four and did not know that Sarah was dead.

Fran declined. For the first time since moving away, Vi was coming home, though only for three days—she and Scott were flying to Santa Barbara with the Edels for New Year's.

Nothing about Vi's appearance comforted Fran. The weight had settled in her bottom. She resembled the pear-shaped cousins she and Sarah had ridiculed as girls. Worse, the remnant of a bruise, now yellow, shaded her chin. She claimed to have collided with the bathroom door in the dark. "He doesn't know how to close a fucking door," she said, then smiled, Fran noted, to mask the anger. Vi could not imagine spending a night away from Scott and slept at the Edels' house. When she invited Fran to Christmas Eve dinner, Fran accepted.

Scott answered the door. His appearance shocked her. He had put on thirty pounds, his belly spilling over his belt like a middle-aged man's. His face was fat, jowls loose, his skin doughy. He was wearing glasses—wire-rimmed things that emphasized his fleshy cheeks. His hair had been cut very short, revealing a high forehead almost converging around a little scrap of stubble.

"Something's wrong with my eyes," he said in response to Fran's stare. "Can't seem to wear my contacts."

It was clear that Vi perceived none of the change. She still saw him as he used to be—the athlete, big sister's pretty boyfriend. A stranger would think him ugly, Fran decided.

During the course of the dinner, Fran found out that he had dropped out of the university. Starting next month he would begin training to become a realtor. He and Vi looked to Fran, their faces bright with anticipation. Was she supposed to be flattered? "There are some names I can call you—some realtors in Tucson," she said, but she was thinking, *It's all downhill for you.*

Vi sat next to him, uncomprehending, the bruise making her face lopsided. The outfit she wore didn't suit her—a shapeless, billowy dress with appliquéd lace in the shape of a heart and short, puffy sleeves—the sort of thing Sarah could carry off, but not Vi.

Scott told a story about a bum they had found one morning sleeping in their yard. "He wasn't anything to be scared of, so we gave him breakfast." He flashed the grotesque tooth. No matter how carefully he framed the story, it circled back to his own generosity. How was it none of the others perceived this as self-congratulatory? "You should have seen the getup he had on," Scott said, and Fran realized, with a start, that the dress Vi wore *was* Sarah's. Sarah and she had purchased it together her senior year.

As if she could read Fran's mind, Vi said, "My clothes don't fit me anymore, Mom." She tugged at the waist. "This is loose, like a parachute. That's what Scottie calls it, the parachute dress."

"It was your sister's," Fran said and resumed eating.

After dinner, they exchanged gifts, as was the custom in the Edel family. The Schaefers opened presents on Christmas Day, so Fran did not feel awkward having come empty-handed. Only when Scott handed her a gift did she realize that she had purchased nothing for him. She asked to wait until morning to open it, reminding them that Lyle was away and there would be few presents under her tree.

She excused herself and left. The only store she could find open was Alpha Beta. She bought Scott a Walkman and wrapped it in brilliant red paper.

Lyle called late that night. "Mother's okay," he said. "I'd fly back now, but the weather here is lousy."

Fran described Scott's girth, the dress, her unwillingness to open the present.

"Forgive the boy," Lyle said.

"I will not."

"Well, then . . . Merry Christmas," he said. "Give my love to Vi." He hesitated. "This anger is going to show on you. You need to let it go."

"I'm not the one with ulcers," she said.

After hanging up, she found the present from Vi and Scott. A soft bundle, awkwardly packaged, which made her certain that Scott had wrapped it. She carefully clipped the tape on the paper and removed a silk blouse, a skirt. She slipped the skirt back inside the paper and repaired the tape.

The blouse she took outside, to the alley, where she flung it to the ground. On her knees, she wiped it in greasy sand, then stood and stomped on it with her shoe. She buried it deep inside the garbage can.

On the day that Vi and Scott were returning from Santa Barbara, there was a crash at the Tucson Airport. Fran heard about it on the car radio: failed landing gear, three dead, others seriously injured. She did not need to listen any longer to know that it was Vi's flight, to know that Scott had finally taken her down.

She veered across traffic and headed toward the freeway. Halfway through the four-hour drive, she thought to call Lyle. "How do you know it's their flight?" he demanded.

"I just know. They were flying back today. I know."

"I'll make some calls," he said, his voice quaking, shaken by her confidence.

When she arrived in Tucson, she did not know where to go. She had been thinking of the airport, but realized that it was foolish to drive there. She pulled into an Exxon station and hurried to the pay phone by the side of the building. Lyle's secretary answered. "Can you hold?" she asked, and music began before Fran could call her an idiot. A few yards away, a young woman in a wheelchair was laboriously removing herself from the women's room. The tail of the girl's green shirt was caught on the doorknob. Her thin legs were bound in a blanket.

"Do you need help?" Fran called to her, and immediately Lyle was on the line.

"They're all right," he said. Fran burst into tears. "Come home," he said.

"I have to see her. How did she escape?"

"It wasn't their flight, Fran. They were already home. Vi was in the shower when the plane crashed. She heard about it on the radio."

"Are you certain?" Fran said.

"I talked to her. She keeps a radio in the shower—it's designed for the shower, so it's safe. I didn't tell her you were driving there already. It would disturb her to know. Come home now."

"I was so sure," Fran insisted. "Are you absolutely—did she say anything else?"

"Nothing we can't discuss later."

"What? What? I knew there was something. You tell me this instant!"

There was a long pause. Fran could hear his steady breathing. The woman in the wheelchair rolled silently past her. Lyle said, "They're getting married. He proposed on the plane. They've set the date."

Fran began nodding. She had been right all along. There had been a disaster.

SPRING

The day before the wedding, Fran called her daughter to say that Lyle had checked himself into the hospital again. Vi was understanding. "We've had a setback here, too," she said. "Scott fell from a ladder. He tore ligaments in his knee. He's in a cast." She put him on the phone.

"I hope Mr. Schaefer is okay," he said. "I don't know what

Vi told you, but I just spaced out for a moment and fell." While
he spoke, the thought entered Fran's mind: she wished that Scott
would die. "If I'd spread my arms, I could have caught myself,"
he went on.

Fran interrupted. "I should get to the hospital. I shouldn't
leave him alone."

Lyle had been listening and was angry. "It's one thing if
you can't stand the thought of going, but using me, lying like
this—"

"Scott is marrying Sarah's sister. How can you possibly be
angry with *me*?"

The wedding photographs came a week later: Vi and Scott
in the judge's chambers, both of them fat, Scott in a cast, Vi in
sagging stockings, the flash reflecting off Scott's balding pate,
creating a bead of light just above his head.

SUMMER

When Fran finally went to Tucson, it was by herself. The day
before, Lyle had driven the company car across a concrete di-
vider, wrenching his back and neck, slashing open his forehead.
"I was on my way to work, same as always," he explained,
"when suddenly I found myself shipwrecked on the median."

Fran assumed that he had been drinking and would have been
angry with him, but she had come to believe that the world
operated through an invisible sort of justice: because she had
used him as an excuse not to visit, now that she was really
going, of course he was unable to come. It was the same principle that enabled her to understand Scott: he lived off his good
fortune too long, and now had to have the worst sort of luck
as his true self was revealed.

An hour into the drive, Fran began to feel feverish. Her head throbbed at the temples, her eyes ached. The desert sun made ordinary objects sparkle and pulse on the windshield. Everything that moved hurt her eyes. As she neared Tucson, the weight and heat of the fever swelled.

Vi and Scott had a new house at the edge of town. Vi emerged from the front door as Fran pulled to the curb. She ran and threw her arms around her mother. As she'd sworn during one of their phone conversations, she had lost weight.

"You look wonderful, Mom. You could pass for a college student."

"You're exaggerating," Fran said. "But *you* look nice."

"Weight Watchers," she said triumphantly. "I have stretch marks, though. They're gross."

She took Fran for a tour of the house. There were three bedrooms and bright shafts of light. A stationary bicycle and a complicated weight-machine for Scott's rehabilitation filled the den, and in almost every room there were aquariums. Fran recalled that Scott liked fish; she remembered shopping with Sarah for neons and betas, the scavenger cats and miniature sharks.

"Scottie's gone to the grocery," Vi told her. "He's cooking tonight."

"Do you have aspirin?" Fran asked her.

"It's practically our middle name," Vi said.

Fran napped. When she woke up, two hours later, her fever had escalated and her body ached. Vi sat in a rattan chair beside the bed reading a novel. "Scott is making you soup," she said. "I'm sorry you're sick."

"Maybe I just need to rest."

"Soup will do you good," Vi said. "We eat soup year-round." She closed her book and pulled her feet into the chair. "I wish Daddy would have come. I wish he could handle this."

Grief

"What do you mean?" Fran asked.

"I wish he could get used to me and Scott," she said. At that moment Scott called to her from another room. "Just a second," she called back. "I wish he'd at least talk to Scott, or, you know, *look* at him." She shook her dark hair as she stood. "I've gotta go help."

Lying in a strange bed, sickly hot, her head pounding, Fran cast back over the past two years. It seemed to her that the time had been consumed by Scott's doings, but there were facts, undeniable facts: Lyle had not seen or spoken with Scott since the accident; he had not seen his only living daughter since she had moved out, more than a year ago. How had she missed this? How had he kept this from her?

A portable phone rested on the nightstand, and she dialed home. "How are you feeling?" she asked.

"A little better," Lyle said. She could hear liquor in his speech. "My forehead started bleeding for some reason during lunch, but it quit. My neck is . . . oh, still some pain."

"When are you going to see your daughter again?"

The phone went quiet. She heard ice cubes rattling in a glass. Finally, he said, "Is it my turn now? I don't think I could bear it, Fran. Are you going to hate *me* now?"

"That's a horrible thing to say."

"My neck hurts," he said, then he added, "I'm drinking. Listen, let's don't get into this now. Let's don't analyze me just yet. All right? Give Vi—" he paused, and she heard the slight whistle of his breath "—Scott, too—give them my love."

"How?" Fran asked. "If you can't stand to be with them, how am I—"

"Think of something, Fran." He sighed. "Use the old noodle." His breathing became suddenly heavy and his voice coarse. "I'm going to lie down. I'm taking it easy today. I'm giving myself the day off from the world."

She returned the phone to its cradle and carefully positioned her head against the feather pillow. Had she said good-bye? She thought she had, but she wasn't certain. "Give them my love," he had said, and she believed that he meant it. He loved them, but he could not face them.

"May I come in?" Scott stepped into the room carrying a tray.

Fran took a quick drag of breath, then coughed to hide her astonishment. The impossible had happened. He had become the old Scott. He looked exactly as he had when he had dated Sarah. His face was thin and handsome, the glasses gone. He wore his hair long again, and it covered his forehead. Even his arms had a muscular tone. "I made you soup," he said, and his voice had the lift and lilt of youth.

This was the boy with whom her daughters had fallen in love. This was Sarah's love. Now Vi's love. Miraculously restored.

Steam rose from the soup, a mixture of vegetables with little chunks of chicken breast. She tasted lime and cilantro. Eating the first bite made her feel instantly better, and with each additional bite the headache receded, the fever and pressure vanquished.

Scott turned his back to her and opened the blinds. It surprised her that there was still daylight. She took another spoonful of the soup—delicious, rejuvenating.

Sunlight through the slats made Scott appear to glow, and this seemed to Fran like a clue. The moment felt suddenly fraught with significance, and she tried to concentrate. Scott paused with his back to her, as if to give her the time to figure it out.

She said, "Lyle sends you his love."

He turned slightly and smiled in response. The ragged tooth had been repaired. He was beautiful.

Facing the window once more, he said, "Sarah died from the fall. I've wanted to tell you this for a long time. I pulled her from the car myself, and she was already gone. She didn't suffer."

"Oh," Fran said softly.

He stood at the window several moments, sunlight pouring over him out of a blue sky. Above one shoulder lay the peaks of distant mountains, the same range of mountains from which he and Sarah had fallen. He raised his arms, pivoting at the waist, apparently stretching, but Fran saw through the gesture. Her secret logic turned a final notch, and she saw the truth.

He was showing her his wings.

Scott was an angel—her angel. The object of her rage. Who bore the crushing weight of their sorrow. Whose body had been deformed by their suffering and had now been restored.

The recognition took her heart as if in a fist, a pressure more painful than anger—the full ache of grief. He had spared her this until now, spared her by surviving the killing fall, which had permitted her to despise him.

She trembled with awareness, her temples throbbing, and she understood that her fever had not passed. The soup merely had given her an excuse for the heat she felt. And Scott stood before her no longer an angel, just a man. She did not feel delirious, but she must have been hallucinating. "Perhaps I should take aspirin again," she said.

Scott turned to her, the sun lighting half his face. He hesitated, about to speak, and although he did not move his lips, Fran heard what she wanted him to say, heard it clearly, as if he had spoken. "I forgive you," he said. "We all forgive you."

Scott's real voice interrupted. "It hasn't been long enough," he said, and Fran felt her heart contract again. Her sudden pained expression made him step toward her. "The directions on the bottle say to wait four hours," he explained. "We've become experts on medication here." He offered her a smile.

She nodded, which made the soup slosh onto the white sheet and soak through her clothing to her skin, a spreading warmth, a feeling something like an approximation of joy, or like a growing stain of fresh, radiant blood.

Living to Be a Hundred

It's fair to say that our house was not in order. Furniture from the living room filled the kitchen. Chairs inverted on chairs surrounded the dining table. A long tan couch, stripped of its cushions, blocked the hall. In our bedroom, beside the dresser, a wooden coffee table stood upright like a basset hound begging for scraps.

On our knees in the emptied living room, we pieced together carpet remnants. I aligned a wide strip of tape, bending low to hold it, my shirt wrinkling against my back like molting skin. Harvis applied heat with Linda's travel iron, while she held the odd-shaped pieces together. We inched across the floor, inhaling the odors of scorched glue, new carpet, our own sweating bodies. An oscillating fan vibrated against the wall every fifteen seconds, the air from it blocked by Mix, our sleeping golden retriever.

"This is not the way I thought it would work," Linda said. She pressed against the upside-down carpet, the material rough and woven like a gunnysack. In the crush of hands, her fingers lay on top of mine, our wedding rings grating. "It's going so slowly." Drops of sweat glistened at the base of her neck and on her chest, the straps of her white blouse turning gray with it. Her hair, gathered in a bun behind her head, had ends like the teeth of a comb, and even they drooped in the heat. "It's going to take forever." Her voice sounded desperate, with an edge that suggested she was about to cry. Ordinarily, Linda was the handy one around the house, fixing the clock radio when the numbers quit rolling, building a box to cover Kitty's litter bed, but putting a carpet together had been my idea. For weeks Harvis and I had collected remnants from the construction site where we worked.

"Maybe we should take a break," I said.

The fan rattled against the wall. Linda shook her head until the noise stopped. "The house is such a mess. We can't quit now." She was twenty-eight, with a sweetly freckled face and hair as blond as running water. We'd met in college, in an archaeology class, which had been my major. She'd studied art history. We had been married seven years and put up with a lot of lousy jobs and bad apartments, but the past couple of years it had become harder because we couldn't see an end to it.

"Damn." Harvis shook his hand in the air. "Burned my pinkie." A bubble of glue coagulated on a finger as thick as a wiener. He put his hands on his knees and straightened his back. Beads of perspiration shone on his forehead. "We won't finish today," he said. "That's clear enough."

The dog groaned at this remark, which made us laugh, and, just like that, we changed our mood and worked happily again.

Linda bought and sold used clothing at a hip secondhand store. Before I got the job working construction, I had been a short-order cook, and before that, a cashier at a convenience market. I was thirty-two. Construction paid best and it wasn't so killing. You know what I mean, killing? The past couple of years had been tough, but I had begun to think things were looking up.

Linda started talking about a woman who had come into the store carrying a black fingertip coat and wanting another just like it. "We don't stock many coats this time of year. I knew I couldn't help her." She ran her hand across the base of her neck as she spoke, wiping the sweat onto her jeans.

Harvis leaned against the iron. "What'd she want with a coat like the one she already had?"

Linda nodded. "That's what I wanted to know."

It seemed obvious to me. "Someone had told her what a nice coat it was, and she wanted to make a gift of one just like it."

"Women don't do that," Harvis said. "They never want anyone to have the same clothes."

"I asked her." Linda pushed a new piece of carpet toward me, leaning low. I could see down her blouse. We slept in the same bed every night, but the sight of her breasts at that moment pleased me as much as it would a teenager. Harvis was looking too. "She wanted to get rid of the coat but couldn't bear to do it until she had another like it. She said she just felt like a change."

I laughed. "Sounds like a nut." I cut another strip of tape. The dog groaned again and rolled onto his back.

"She didn't look like one," Linda said. "She looked very normal."

"You can't tell a nut by its shell." Harvis smiled at his joke. Then he jerked his hand away from the iron. "Life is too much," he said and stuck his thumb in his mouth.

"Let me iron for a while." I pushed him out of the way. "You aren't going to have any fingers left."

"I'm going to make some iced tea." Linda smiled as she stood. We were all happy, even Harvis with his burned fingers.

I shoved the scraps that we hadn't used into a corner, making a path from the front door to the kitchen. There was no point in moving the furniture back. We were only half-finished. The movie theater down the street offered a discount during the afternoon, and we had decided to get out of the heat and away from the mess. Harvis showered first, then took Mix on a walk.

"That was almost fun," Linda said, her back to the shower nozzle, water spraying off her head in all directions. "It was almost awful, too." Her teeth were as white as the porcelain.

"It'll be nice once we're through," I said. "And we could never afford it otherwise."

"You don't have to convince me." She rubbed soap on my chest. A year earlier, after a Sunday of sweating and only half-finishing, we would have been angry with each other. We would have blamed and accused. Linda ran the bar of soap across my stomach, down my thighs, and kissed me.

"Harvis is a good friend," she said, soaping me now between my legs, and kissing me again, so that the only way I had to agree was to nod.

"We can save Harvis a seat." Linda stood in the hall, tucking a purple T-shirt into a pair of khaki shorts. The couch separated us. She combed her wet hair with her fingers. "I can't stand this."

Kitty was in her box, wailing. She was an old cat, a present that Linda had been given for her fifteenth birthday. Over the course of the past year almost everything had become painful for her. Linda had built the box to reduce odor, but it had become the container for such yowls of anguish that each time the cat entered we were afraid she would not come out.

Linda crawled across the couch, and just as we opened the front door, the wailing stopped. Kitty padded across the room and out to the porch, where she leaped to the railing, stretched, and closed her eyes. Linda rubbed the cat's belly. "Lazy Kitty," she said, then stepped down from the porch and to the hibiscus bush, which was in bloom. The flowers were red and long, shaped like the end of a bugle. She put one behind her ear, giggling.

Down the hill, Harvis approached, hands in his pockets, Mix loping beside him, leash trailing the ground. Harvis saw this as a way of getting around the leash law. He liked circumventing rules. While we watched, Mix abruptly lifted his head and darted into the street. A yellow cat streaked across the pavement to a utility pole. Mix, as usual, arrived late, barking and standing on his hind legs. The cat climbed straight up the pole.

"That's why there's a leash law," Linda called out so that Harvis could hear.

He had already grabbed the dog by the collar and pulled him away. "Mix wouldn't hurt anything."

"You better hurry," I said. "We'll miss the start of the movie."

Then everyone was in motion. Harvis and Mix ran to the house, while Linda and I walked toward the pole. "Hey, cat," Linda called. "You can come down now." The cat looked at us but kept climbing. "Here, kitty," she said. "Here, kitty, kitty." The yellow cat reached the transformer box and stepped onto it.

"Maybe she needs to turn around," I said, but Linda kept calling. Meanwhile, Kitty had jumped down from the porch railing and obediently trotted down the hill.

"Did you think I was calling you?" Linda said. She retrieved Kitty and began walking back to the house, passing Harvis, who had bolted out of the door to catch us.

"You're going the wrong way," he said.

At that moment, high above me—a loud electric snap. I spun around, raising my arms. The yellow cat paused in midair, three feet above the transformer box, before beginning her fall to the asphalt. She bounced once, then lay still.

Linda screamed. She looked at me in disbelief, as if it were I who had fallen. "God," she said, her voice squeaking, and ran into the house. Harvis stood on the pavement like a statue, his hands suspended above his waist, legs spread as if he were about to run.

Here's what I couldn't decide: Should I go to the cat or to my wife? The cat surely was dead. My wife was crying. What comfort can you give the dead? I wish that was all there was to my decision, but there was also this: I didn't want to touch a thing so newly dead.

Linda knelt on a pile of carpet scraps, crying, stroking Kitty. "How could that happen? How bad is it hurt?"

"It's dead. The shock killed it." I dropped to one knee and touched her back. "Or maybe the fall."

"I should have kept Mix on the leash." Harvis stood by the door, hands in his pockets.

"It was a freak thing," I said. "We should get a trash bag. We shouldn't leave it out there."

"A box," Linda said, leaving me, stepping over another mound of carpet and then onto the couch, ducking her head as she crossed into the hall. She returned with a cardboard box from our bedroom closet.

From the porch, Linda watched Harvis and me walk back down the street, but the cat was gone. "Jesus," I said and knelt as if it were still there. A tiny square of blood marked the asphalt. "I was sure it was dead."

"It must be in terrible pain," Harvis said.

"They hide," Linda called as she ran toward us. "When they're hurt or something's wrong, they find a place to hide."

We searched under cars and porch steps, beneath an old tub in a neighbor's yard, inside a tipped garbage can. I lifted a sheet of plywood that leaned against the side of an adobe house. A black-and-white cat stared at me, nothing like the one who had fallen. We searched separately until dark, and we returned separately, Linda several steps ahead, arms crossed as if against a chill, and I thought what little it took to throw your life off, to turn it upside down.

"Castellani," Johansson said to me. "Tella truth. You think any of these punks they got fighting today could stand up to Joe Louis? Or Ezzard Charles? Ingemar Johansson? Tella truth, what you think?"

We sat together for lunch in what little shade the skeletal building offered—Johansson, Lernic, Harvis, and I. There used to be more of us, but this was a desert town and it dried out in the summer, everyone going away, out of the heat. Then Graham was fired for drinking and Iglesia was deported. The apartments were almost completed. Our crew stayed small.

"I don't follow boxing," I said and finished off the sandwich I'd thrown together before leaving for work. It had been a bad night, Linda and I with no place to sit but the bed, nothing to do but the carpet, and neither of us willing to work on that. Harvis had gone home, but I'd wished that he'd stayed for a while. Sometimes he made it easier for us to be together. Linda, I'm pretty sure, had felt the same.

"They couldn't hold Ingemar's mouthpiece," Johansson said. "He's practically a relative of yours truly, more or less, like we'd be cousins if he lived around here." Johansson was in charge of us, a red-faced little man who wore long-sleeve plaid shirts rolled to the elbows. "And he could punch. You ever seen those films of him whupping Patterson? Tella truth, you ever seen such a punch? On my father's side, we all been fighters."

Johansson and Lernic sat on the tailgate of a company truck. Harvis and I reclined against concrete, the foundation for the apartments. Drywallers worked down the site from us, where we'd been the week before. At the far end were painters and carpet layers. Eventually it would be a big complex. The pool was already in.

"I like to watch girls fight," Lernic said. "They don't have rules for that." His face was big, sloppy; his skin, the color and texture of angel food cake. "Rip those clothes, Mama. Yank that hair. Bite that tit." He laughed and leaned back on his elbows. "Harvis was a boxer, I bet. Big and dumb enough. Fag enough. You a boxer, Harvis?"

"Fuck off," Harvis said.

"Scratch you like a girl, I bet." Lernic laughed again. "Big old nothing Harvis rip at your shirt. 'Let me at them titties. Let me at them titties.' " Lernic waggled his fingers at Johansson's shirt, then leaned back again. "Bite this, Harvis." He gripped the crotch of his pants.

I stood and nudged Harvis on the shoulder. "Let's walk off lunch. We've got fifteen minutes."

"He don't mean nothing," Johansson said. "Tell them you don't mean nothing, Lernic. It's his way of being funny."

Lernic's hand was still at his crotch. "Watch your step, Castellani. That big fag'll cornhole you in the behind."

"That's redundant," I said, walking away. "Like saying Lernic the dumbass."

"There you go," Johansson said. "Everybody's got a way of being funny."

"That guy makes me crazy," Harvis said, throwing his thumb over his shoulder when we'd walked far enough away.

"Screw Lernic," I said. "You let assholes get to you and your life is shit."

"I'm supposed to act like he doesn't exist?"

"He's a pathetic boob."

"You've got Linda," Harvis said. "You can say that stuff. I've got to take boobs seriously. I could wind up one. Hell, I could be one already. You've got Linda. You can let the rest go."

"So, you've got me *and* Linda," I said.

"See?" Harvis put one of his big fingers square in my chest. "That's just the kind of thing you say to a pathetic boob. See there?"

After lunch I took off my shirt. That was one of the things I liked about the job. I could take off my shirt and work on the high boards, stepping from scaffolding to beam. And the smell of lumber. The pull and give of my muscles. The paycheck.

I had planned to be an archaeologist, although I know now I might as well have planned to be an astronaut. "You can be whatever you want," my mother had told me, "whatever you put your heart into." A good-natured lie. I could not be an archaeologist—not and make enough money to eat.

Our plan, Linda's and mine, had been for her to go to graduate school to become a librarian. It wasn't exactly what she'd wanted, but it sounded all right to her. Then she'd get a job and I'd study archaeology again, give it a shot. That was why we'd moved here, near a university. There was nothing wrong with our plan, but we couldn't make it work. At first we needed Linda's income to get by. Then we bought a television on time. We went to the movies. Sometimes we went out and ate steak. We didn't sell out our dreams—we siphoned them off.

Construction was better than cooking burgers, a lot better, but once, years ago, I went as a student on a dig in Mexico, and with a whisk and an air brush, I uncovered a clay jar, a carved spoon, the curved line of a jawbone. I studied people by looking at what had endured. At the ruins of Palenque, I climbed to the opening in the temple, then descended dark stairs, turned a narrow corner, and there was the sepulchral slab, covering the body of an ancient priest. What I felt was wonder, and no matter how many nails I pounded or boards I sawed, I could not claim wonder at seeing a building built. There were some who could; I was not among them. My life hadn't worked out the way I'd planned.

"Johansson," Lernic yelled, even though Johansson was only a few feet away.

I looked down at them. Lernic, on his knees, marked a sheet of plywood. Johansson and Harvis unloaded lumber from the truck.

"You see that show on TV last night?" Lernic said. "I almost forgot. You see it?"

"My television gets nothing but static these days. Lot like you, Mr. Lernic." Johansson backed away from the truck with an armload of two-by-fours. Harvis lifted the other end.

"It was educational, Mr. Johansson. And you could have used it to save one of your employees—Mr. Harvis. You do have a Mr. Harvis working for you?" He quit marking the plywood and stared at Johansson, as if Harvis wasn't there. I could see it all from the second-story scaffolding.

"Go to fucking hell," Harvis said.

"Lay off," Johansson said.

"I got something to tell you, goddamn it." Lernic stood and faced Harvis. "This guy on TV said you can die from screwing nothing but your hand, and here I am trying to save your worthless life, and you got no gratitude."

Harvis dropped his end of the lumber. The boards rattled against the tailgate. "You fuck," he said and stepped toward him.

Lernic picked up the circular saw and revved it once. "Come on, meat. Come get carved."

"Put that down," Johansson said. "Quit being funny. You wanna keep your job, you put that down."

Lernic turned his head from Harvis to Johansson and back to Harvis. For an instant, none of us moved.

I lifted the hammer from my belt and let it drop near Lernic's feet. He jumped, then smiled up at me. "Huh," he grunted, put down the saw, and went back to work.

I couldn't hate Lernic, although I wanted to. There had been a day, only a couple of weeks back, when Harvis was down with the flu and staying at our house because his cooler was out and he had no television. I had gone home at lunch break to have a bowl of soup with him and was ten minutes late getting back. I didn't want Lernic to have anything else to throw at Harvis, so I said it was Linda who was sick.

Johansson let it go, but Lernic, of course, didn't.

"You pussy-whipped bastard. Worst case I've ever seen," he said. He'd met Linda when she used to take me to work, before I knew Harvis well enough to ride with him.

That same afternoon Johansson told us about a book he'd like to write, *The Life and Legend of Ingemar Johansson*. "I got the first sentence. That's the hardest part. You listen a this," he said. "Every man has a day in his life when nobody can defeat him, and that day for Ingemar Johansson happened when he was fighting for the heavyweight championship of the world." He beamed. "You read that sentence, who's gonna be able to stop? I figure I write about that whole idea, how everybody gets one day when they're the best. Ingemar, he got his day when he had the big fight. That'sa difference between a great man and one a us."

"Shit," Lernic said.

"No," Johansson said. "Really, what you think? Most people, they get their day, they probably sleep through it or lay around drunk. A Johansson don't. He gets the fight of his life."

Lernic snorted. "You're not related to any champion, and you know it."

"We got the same name."

"A name don't mean shit."

"Name's as good as anything. Tella truth, if they'd been a Ingemar Lernic who whupped Joe Frazier, say. You'd be proud as two peacocks."

"The only guy who could have beaten Frazier was just what beat him: another big, dumb nigger. I'm going to be proud because I got the same name as a big dumb nigger?" Lernic hammered against a board three times, as if in answer to his question.

"Names mean a lot," Johansson said. "Castellani, tella truth. If there was a Ingemar Castellani, you'd be proud as two peacocks."

"You never called anybody a nigger when Graham worked here," I said to Lernic.

"So? He was a nigger. You think I'm stupid?" He raised the hammer to pound the board again. There were no nails in the board.

"Names must mean something," I said.

"You see there." Johansson waggled a knobby finger. "Now that's settled. We got work to do."

Johansson walked away, but Lernic put his hand on my shoulder. "Your wife is pretty," he said. He looked at me as if I should understand something. "I know all about it." He squeezed my shoulder slightly, then looked at Johansson's back for a second. "The hardest thing for a man is to be a man and still keep a woman." He dropped his hand to the head of his hammer, which rode in his carpenter's belt. "I just thought I'd say that."

"Yeah," I said. "Okay."

He lifted the hammer to eye level, staring at it self-consciously. For an instant I saw it as an archaeologist might hundreds of years from now, how the blunt black head and sweeping rear prongs resembled the head of a dragon.

"We got work to do," Lernic said, and since then, I couldn't hate him, much as I tried.

Harvis and I arrived at the house before Linda did. The living room, the mess of carpet and tape, and the kitchen, the tangle of chairs around Kitty's box, kept us from entering. We sat on the front porch, stalling until she arrived.

"We can't seem to face it," I said as she walked up the porch steps.

She shielded her eyes with her hands and looked into the window. "This is a test." She spoke somberly, her lips inches from the glass. "A trial of some sort." Linda believed in god, not a man with a gray beard, but a force that gave reason to being. "If we can get through this, it'll mean something."

"If we can get through this, it'll mean there is no intelligent life on this planet," I said.

Harvis shook his big head. "If we get through this, it'll mean we'll live to be a hundred."

Linda turned from the window. She wasn't smiling. "Let's go somewhere and have a beer," she said.

Harvis chucked his thumb toward the window. "I left some in the refrigerator."

"I know that." She stepped from the porch and we followed.

We had pepperoni pizza with extra sauce and drank beer by the pitcher. Harvis told us how he used to be a mugger. "It's the truth," he said. "For about a week. I wasn't any good at it." I wanted to know what made him do it. Linda wanted to know what made him quit.

"I was broke and living in this little dump in Chicago, and my head was all turned around every which way, and I couldn't get a job, and I couldn't think straight, and I'd see these women by themselves or with little kids, and they all had purses, and all I had to do was go and yank it away and run off, and there it was." Harvis, when he drank, rambled.

"You were a purse snatcher," Linda said. "That's not the same as a mugger."

"Whatever you call it, it was low, and I felt mean about it, but I couldn't get turned around the right way until one day I was out in the park and along comes a young woman carrying a bundle with both arms and a big purse hanging from her elbow, one of those hippy bags, and I figured she wouldn't have much money, but I could just run by and grab the purse and keep on running, and I didn't need all that much money—you see, I was all turned around in my head, but I wasn't greedy." He took an enormous drink from his glass, filled it again, and took another big drink. He emptied the pitcher, then tapped it against the table, holding it as if it were a mug, tapping it as if it were a gavel.

"I ran right up to her, and I had my hand out to rip off her purse, and just then she turned to me, and stared right at me, and she said, 'I need to find the hospital. My baby has died.' " He brought the pitcher down again, breaking it, the handle remaining in his hand, the pitcher falling into his lap. His palm began to bleed. "My head wasn't on straight, and I didn't know what was up, and I didn't know what was down, and that little baby was no bigger than a football, and I wanted to do something good for that woman, and you know, I couldn't think of anything, except taking her to the hospital, which is what I did."

Linda reached into his lap and retrieved the pitcher. She kissed him on the forehead and on the cheek.

* * *

Each night we found a reason not to work on the carpet, or we worked for half an hour then sat next to the fan and drank beer and talked. Friday morning, I stepped out of the shower, and Linda lay over the arm of the couch in the hall, crying. I tried to lift her to me, but she didn't want to be held. "We'll finish this tomorrow," I said, "if it takes all day and night." She just crawled across the couch.

After work, Harvis drove me to the florist, then dropped me off at the secondhand store, where I waited in our car until Linda was free. We went out to eat, then drove to a motel.

What I'm saying is that I knew there was real danger. I was trying to ward it off.

The motel room was a pastel yellow. A painting of the ocean at night hung above our bed. The air conditioner, which lined the wall beneath the window, hummed and chortled like a friendly drunk. We crawled under the sheets and watched a movie on television. A red-headed woman walked briskly down a city street, wearing a red blouse, red skirt, red shoes. She practically skipped. Linda put her hand on my chest. "How can we afford this?" It was the first thing either of us had said for a long time.

"We needed to get out of the house." I spoke softly and touched her hair. "We can fix it tomorrow. Tonight we needed to get out."

"We could have stayed with Harvis," she said. "We didn't have to spend all this money."

"This is better," I said.

The woman, in an office now, lifted her red blouse over her head, untied her red skirt, and she was naked. It startled me, like going to a friend's house and a stranger answers the door.

"This must be cable." Linda leaned forward in the bed. "Do you think she's pretty?"

"I don't know," I said, although she was obviously very pretty.

"She is," Linda said. The woman walked around the office in high heels. A man behind a desk smoked a cigar as he watched her. "Why do you think Harvis can't get a girlfriend?"

"I don't know that he can't. He just doesn't. He's shy around women."

Linda crossed her arms across her breasts. We were naked, and I had been hoping we would make love. "He's not shy around me," she said.

"He knows you."

The woman stepped behind the desk and began undressing the man.

"Are they going to show everything?" Linda said. "Are they going to do it? Is this that kind of movie?"

We watched the man and woman make love. The camera moved in close and then backed away.

"They're really doing it." Linda raised herself to her knees and watched. I ran my hand along her leg, but she took it in her palms, patted it gently just the way she pats Mix, then placed it back at my side. "You know who would enjoy this?" she said. "You know what would be fun?"

"That's not a good idea," I said.

"I'll just call and tell him about it." She had already moved toward the phone. "We haven't seen him all day."

"I worked with him eight hours. He took me to the florist. He drove me to the store." She had begun to dial. I reached between her arms and stopped the call.

Linda dropped the receiver and walked to the window. She peeked through the curtains. "Oh," she said softly, and I thought she said something more.

"Come back to bed." I sat on the edge.

She faced me, my beautiful wife, naked, almost crying. "Let me do what I want."

"I've been with him all day. I don't want to see Harvis." Before I could say anything else, she opened the door and stepped outside.

The night was warm. Cicadas rattled. The sky was dark as if blackened by fire. She stood with her back to me in the parking lot. I dragged the bedspread and threw it over both of us. Her fingers locked around my neck, elbows at my chest. We rested forehead to forehead. "Did you feed Mix?" she whispered. "Did you put something out for Kitty?"

"Harvis said he'd take care of it. He wanted to walk Mix."

Tears appeared on her lashes. "I'm all turned around inside," she said. Whether she knew she was echoing Harvis, I'm not sure. "I want to run through this parking lot naked. I want to scream and wake up everyone. I want to hit you. I want this off of me." She yanked the bedspread down. "I want to stand in the middle of the street and shout the meanest things I can think of. I want to leave you." She tried to pull away from me, but I had a good grip around her waist.

"We'll go back inside." I jerked her even closer. "You can call anyone you want."

She shook her head once, sharply. But she came with me and turned off the television and turned off the lights and lay near me in the dark until she could sleep.

We woke up early and drove home. Harvis got there at eight, work time. He had Mix with him. "You let this dog sleep in bed with you? He's a bed hog. Almost nuzzled me to the floor."

"You want coffee?" I asked.

"Yeah." He petted Mix and looked to Linda. "He farts, too."

She laughed and pointed at me. "He won't let him on our bed."

"I don't blame him," Harvis said. "There's too much dog in this dog."

By ten it was sweltering. We worked steadily, switching jobs, crawling across the floor. Linda and I were in shorts; our knees and elbows burned. We had used all the big scraps, and now pieced together the small ones, which took longer and accomplished less.

"Maybe we don't have enough to make it," Linda said. She sounded hopeful.

"We've got plenty," Harvis said.

"We've got enough for the hall, too," I added, but she didn't laugh.

We ate lunch on the porch, sitting on the rough, sun-dried planks, our backs against the railing. The odor of hibiscus, normally sweet, smelled like smoke, as if cooked by the sun.

"This is good." Harvis waved his egg salad sandwich, his arm brilliant with sweat.

"Oh yeah?" Linda said. "You must have something different from mine. Let me have a bite."

"No way," he said.

She grabbed his arm and tried to wrestle it toward her. "A bite. A bite," she said, laughing, pressing her cheek against his bicep.

"Forget it," he said.

She leaned into him hard and pulled on his slick arm.

"I'll get it." I tried to sound conspiratorial. Before I could snatch the sandwich she threw herself on top of Harvis and dug her face into the smashed sandwich. Egg salad covered her mouth and cheeks, the bridge of her nose. "Delicious," she said, lifting her head. She wiped off her chin and offered me the finger. When I parted my lips, she pressed her finger deep into my mouth.

*   *   *

At two-thirty Harvis and I crept across the couch to the bedroom and searched through drawers until I found gym shorts that fit him. His jeans had become unbearable. We crawled back and worked barechested. "Cheats," Linda said when we took off our shirts. She pulled off her shoes and socks, then wiped her face with the tail of her T-shirt. Her bare stomach startled me as the television had the night before. She saw my face, looked to Harvis, who had his nose in the carpet, then lifted the T-shirt higher, wiping her forehead and exposing her white breasts.

My heart beat against my chest like a paddle.

By three, we knew we would not finish before dark, probably not even if we worked well into the night. A screech came from the kitchen, from Kitty's box, a scale of pain.

"I can't stand it," Linda said. She ran to the couch, ducked low, and disappeared down the hall.

"I'm a fool," I said. A rash had begun on my chest. The cat's cry flattened, then lifted again.

"Give me some more tape," Harvis said.

We heard the shower begin. We fitted more carpet and ironed. When Linda stepped off the couch, she had on a clean white T-shirt and the bottom half of her black bikini. Her wet breasts showed through the shirt like the mounds of a relief map.

We worked as if under water, each movement deliberate and unreal. Harvis pointed at my rash and put his shirt back on, but I knew and Linda knew that it was to hide his erection. He turned his back to us to button the shirt. I looked at Linda and shook my head. It was the wrong thing to do.

She touched Harvis's thigh. He was on his knees facing away, hands still at his buttons. "Linda," I whispered, as if she would hear and not Harvis. She touched his thigh above the knee, lightly, then moved up his leg. He stared at the wall. Her fingers reached the bottom of the gym shorts, ran along the narrow hem. For an instant, none of us moved.

I wish I could say that I yanked her hand away or that I burst into tears, but there was a trembling inside me, a vacillation of spirit. Some part of me wanted to see her fingers continue their climb up his leg, and that part kept the rest of me silent for the long seconds that followed, until Linda pulled her hand away.

We worked another twenty minutes. "I'll make iced tea," Linda said, almost a whisper, but she did not go to the kitchen. She crawled onto the couch and down the hall.

Harvis stood and stared at the doorway where she had just vanished. "I've never wanted anything so bad in my life," he said, then wiped the sweat from his face. I stood and he put his arm around me. "Do something," he said. "Do something fast." He hugged me for an instant. I felt his erection against my hip. He picked up his jeans and left.

I waited for her, expecting her to appear in just the T-shirt. Or less. When she stepped off the couch, she was wearing an old pair of trousers and a blue workshirt. Her eyes were red, her face mottled.

"Harvis had to go," I said.

"Oh." She looked at her pants. "I've been crying."

"It's been tough today."

She nodded. "Do you think we should quit or stick it out?"

My heart pounded again. "I can do a lot myself, if you're tired."

She shook her head and knelt beside me to return to the hard work.

* * *

Near dawn, we glued the final fragment into place and flipped the carpet-side up—a difficult maneuver—then inched it into the corners, pushing and pulling, flattening. We lay side by side on the carpet we'd made. She put her head against my shoulder.

"We should have bought a mat to go beneath it," she said. "It looks so good. How long will it last without a mat? A year? Two years?"

"It could last a long time," I said.

She rose and turned off the light, then lay beside me again in the dark. "This was a test."

"No, it wasn't." I closed my eyes. "This was just one of those things."

"Oh, is that what this was?" She whispered this in my ear, laughing gently. "I want to sleep here tonight."

I nodded, and our long fatigue settled us one against the other, letting us sleep.

Almost a month later, Harvis and I were asked to work a Saturday for time-and-a-half pay. The smallness of our crew had permitted the drywallers to catch up.

Johansson refused on principle. "They don't want this thing built," he told us. "They just want us to fry out there. I worked construction thirty years. I don't gotta take this. My kid could do better than this. Tella truth, boys, you ever seen such a mess?"

I worked the high boards, pounding a ten-penny nail through a two-by-four into a four-by-four column. I had taken my shirt off. The rash was gone.

Harvis and Lernic hammered beneath me. Hungover, Lernic had been quiet the first hour, but once he started, he talked as if it was all that kept him standing. He talked as if his life depended on it.

"How far up your ass do you shove this hammer every night, Harvis? I'm taking a scientific survey. Three inches? Six inches? I suppose it depends on which end goes in first."

Harvis handled him by being mute, which seemed to push Lernic on. I tried to speak for him, but it did no good. Maybe Johansson could have stopped it. He had the power to fire.

We would quit at noon, I thought. We'd go home and eat with Linda and not return. At ten-twenty, I stepped from the scaffolding to the crossbeams. Below me, between my legs, were the two of them, Harvis, like me, hitting a nail, Lernic looking up.

"Castellani," Lernic said, "settle something for me. That wife of yours, Linda?"

I stared at him and nodded.

"She do fags like Harvis here, or . . ."

Harvis's hammer swung away from its board, a backhanded swing of the dragon-head hammer, the blood from Lernic's forehead a sudden hibiscus bloom. His knees gave simultaneously, and he fell to them, and then to the cement, where his body began quivering, and the life shook out of him.

The nail I'd been hammering still stuck out half an inch. My arm swelled with the next swing. That was my position in it: Would I hit the nail while Lernic bled beneath me?

I did not.

"Give me an hour," Harvis said. "I can get to Mexico."

"I'll try," I said.

"Life's too much." He unbuckled his carpenter's belt, letting it fall, the hammer still in his hand.

I nodded, clinging now to the column, arms tight around it.

"Explain to Linda," he said. "Make her understand. As best you can."

I said, "Check his pulse, Harvis."

Harvis shook his head. "He's dead."

"Check it, Harvis."

"I don't want to touch the bastard."

"We have to make sure he's dead," I said. "He could still be alive."

Harvis knelt over Lernic, his knee in the red puddle. He raised his hammer high.

"No!" I yelled it.

Harvis threw the hammer past me. I ducked, but it missed me by a few feet.

"Some things you don't ask," he said, and he ran to his car.

I stayed up there a while. Lernic's blood made a big pool. I had to be careful getting down.

The police kept me a couple of hours. Johansson was called. He put on a coat and tie and drove over, his hair greased flat against his head and perfectly parted, a gesture of respect, I guess, for the dead, or for the police. "The deceased was a no good who liked ta cause trouble," he said. "He was asking for something like this all-a his life." They wanted to know where Harvis might have run. I told them he'd lived in Chicago, that he might have family there, or friends. It wasn't exactly a lie. They didn't hassle me too much. They believed me when I said that I was on the high boards when it happened.

I walked home.

I could tell you about the walk, the alleys I deliberately took, the broken glass and rotting fruit, the sweating magazines peeking out of trash lids. I could tell you how, when I finally came down to earth, I tried to pinpoint the moment when my life had turned wrong, and how I came to decide that I never should have married Linda, that I should have struggled to pursue my obsessions, that I had been made a coward by love.

I would make my life over, I decided. I would let Linda leave me. I could tell you about my plans, grand ones and petty ones, but when I came out of the alley near our house I saw Linda in the afternoon sun. She was in the grass on her hands and knees. Her hair was thrown over her head to dry, the way women for generations have dried their hair, a position as time-less as the curve of bone. The back of her neck was white and smooth, an exposed and vulnerable swatch. A thing of wonder.

A Note About the Author

Robert Boswell was born in Sikeston, Missouri, and was educated at the University of Arizona in Tucson. His previous work includes the novels *Mystery Ride*, *Crooked Hearts*, and *The Geography of Desire* and a collection of stories, *Dancing in the Movies*. His fiction has appeared in *The New Yorker*, *Esquire*, *Best American Short Stories*, and *O. Henry Prize Stories*. He is an associate professor of English at New Mexico State University, and teaches in the Warren Wilson Master of Fine Arts Program for Writers. He lives with his wife, writer Antonya Nelson, and their children in Las Cruces, New Mexico, and Telluride, Colorado.

A Note on the Type

This book was set in Janson. The hot-metal version of Janson was a recutting made direct from type cast from matrices long thought to have been made by the Dutchman Anton Janson, who was a practicing type founder in Leipzig during the years 1668–1687. However, it has been conclusively demonstrated that these types are actually the work of Nicholas Kis (1650–1702), a Hungarian, who most probably learned his trade from the master Dutch type founder Dirk Voskens.

Composed by Creative Graphics, Allentown, Pennsylvania. Printed and bound by Arcata Graphics, Martinsburg, West Virginia. Designed by Peter A. Andersen.